HONOR CODE

BLACKTHORN SECURITY BOOK 2

GEMMA FORD

Honor Code

Copyright © 2024 by Gemma Ford

All rights reserved.

No part of this book may be reproduced in any form or by any electronic or mechanical means, including information storage and retrieval systems, without written permission from the author, except for the use of brief quotations in a book review.

Mortlake Press

ISBN: 978-1-7385403-3-4

First Edition

Cover design by Deranged Doctor

Disclaimer: This is a work of fiction. Names, characters, places, and incidents are the products of the author's imagination or used in a fictitious manner. Any resemblance to actual persons, living or dead, or actual events is purely coincidental.

CHAPTER 1

*I*t was pitch dark when Ellie opened her eyes. The long-haul flight from Europe had left her tired and cranky and this bed wasn't anything to write home about. She groaned—jetlag could be a bitch.

Reaching over, she checked the time on her phone.

Five a.m.

Was it too early for a yoga session?

Her whole body ached. She desperately needed to stretch out the kinks. Her yoga mat stood in the corner by the door, beckoning to her.

Suzi, her roommate, was still fast asleep, her breathing deep and rhythmic. Careful not to wake her, Ellie slid out of bed, pulled on some leggings and a T-shirt, then grabbed her yoga mat. After scraping her hair back into a ponytail, she snuck out of the room.

The corridors on the oil rig were dark and eerie, bathed in that familiar ghostly green light that cast long shadows on the steel walls. The first time she'd been on an offshore platform, she'd been unnerved by the ethereal glow, but after five years of working in the field, she was used to it.

She made her way up the narrow steel stairway to the top deck, expecting to see some signs of life, but the place was deserted. Then again, it was stupid o'clock and the first shift only begun at eight.

The tropical air caressed her skin, warm and serene—so different from the frigid conditions in the North Sea where she'd worked before. She closed her eyes and let the balmy breeze wash over her, savoring the moment.

With her mat tucked under her arm, she ventured along the gangway, navigating around the now-silent steel structure, with its cranes, multi-level platforms, and columns of drilling equipment, in search of a tranquil corner in which to exercise.

At the railing, she paused and gazed out over the Gulf of Mexico. The dark expanse stretched for miles in all directions. It never failed to move her, the idea that she was a tiny dot in the middle of an enormous ocean. Maybe it was because nobody could get to her out here. She was safe. Protected by thousands of miles of water.

At least she'd thought she was. That was until Suzi had mentioned the recent threat from eco-terrorists. This was a very sensitive area of the Gulf, ecologically fragile, and there were strict protocols in place. She'd read the impact assessments before she'd come out here.

If she'd known about the risk, she might have thought twice before accepting the job.

After what had happened last time...

No, she wasn't going to go there. Ellie took a steadying breath. This project was different. Eco-terrorists chained themselves to structures, got in the way, temporarily disrupted operations. They didn't threaten anyone's personal safety.

Even so, the threat did explain the presence of the armed

patrols she'd seen yesterday when she'd arrived on the helicopter from Corpus Christi. Two enormous security operatives, rifles slung over their broad shoulders, standing watch on the deck. They'd been hard to miss, such was the attention they commanded. Their tight-fitting black T-shirts over rippling muscles had proved at least a five-minute distraction. But despite appearances, or maybe because of it, they'd put her mind at ease.

Tiredness made her neck stiff, and she stretched it out before wandering over to the helipad, the flattest, clearest space she could find. It was deserted, the chopper yet to return.

Perfect.

Ellie rolled out her mat and was just standing upright when a sudden gust of wind made her spin around. In an instant, she was blindsided and taken down hard. Her breath whooshed out of her as she was flattened on the deck.

Panic surged through her.

No! Not again.

She thrashed and squirmed, trying to throw off her attacker, but he had her pinned to the ground. A thousand terrifying thoughts stampeded through her head, scrambling her brain. Blood pumped in her ears, adding to her confusion.

"Get off me!" Her high-pitched cry shattered the early morning quiet.

SHE WAS BACK IN BOSTON, *standing in Raphael's apartment, his arm tight around her waist. The sharp edge of the blade he held pressed against her throat. Cold, uncompromising. One small slash, and she'd bleed out.*

"Don't move," he hissed in her ear.

3

She couldn't; she was too terrified.

"Put down the knife," the police officer ordered, pointing his firearm at them. At Raphael, who used her as his shield. She was the one who'd get shot. The bullet would probably go right through her and hit Raphael too, but she didn't want to put it to the test.

Hot tears stung her eyes. "Rafe, please."

"Shut up," he growled, the blade digging deeper into her skin. A warm trickle dripped down her neck. She was bleeding.

Oh, God. I'm going to die.

That was all she could think about. She'd never see her family again and would die in Raphael's living room, either by his hand or a police bullet. Either way, death loomed, just seconds away.

A HAND, large and suffocating, clamped over her mouth. In the dim pre-dawn light, her attacker was just a shape, an indistinct mass overpowering her. She kicked out, connecting with a soft body part, and heard a satisfying grunt of pain.

No way. This was not happening.

She would not be a victim—again.

The subsequent years of self-defense training kicked in, and she fought with every fiber of her being, scratching, kicking and bucking to get away. But he was strong and countered her desperate thrusts. Finally, her knee connected with his groin, and he swore under his breath, yet his grip remained unyielding.

What did it take to unseat this monster?

Suddenly, he shifted his weight, settling on her pelvis. Massive hands forced her arms above her head. Her T-shirt rode up, exposing her midriff—she could feel the air on her skin. Oh, God. Was he going to rape her?

Trapped, she opened her mouth to scream.

"Don't," came a gruff command, chilling in its calmness. "I just want to talk."

Pinned down, the hard ground of the helipad pressing into her back, she glared angrily up at the man who'd shattered her early morning peace, along with her nerves.

Who the hell was he?

And what did he want with her?

CHAPTER 2

"*W*ho are you?" Phoenix growled, securing the intruder with his full weight. She was light; it wasn't hard to subdue her, but she'd caught him by surprise. He hadn't expected such a frenzied attack.

Damn if his groin didn't throb where the hellcat had kicked him, and she'd left claw marks down his forearm. The woman had fought like her life depended on it.

He could tell she was trained, but not by any military—he knew that much. Not a serious threat, then. Maybe an eco-warrior? One of those passionate planet defenders who didn't realize the danger they put themselves in.

"What's your name?" he repeated. He'd been warned there had been threats. They'd been told to be vigilant.

She squirmed beneath him, but he held her steady, pressing her wrists into the hard ground. Both her hands in one of his. The other he splayed across her hip, preventing her from unseating him with her repeated thrusts.

He regretted the use of force, but she wasn't going anywhere until she'd answered some questions.

"Ellie," she gasped, and he noticed—more than noticed—the way her T-shirt twisted under her breasts, exposing her smooth, flat stomach. It was soft under his hand—he didn't know skin could be that soft.

He forced his gaze to her face—pretty and heart-shaped, with an angry flush staining her cheeks. Her hair had come loose from the binding, splaying out around her.

She lifted her chin, and it was then he noticed the small, inch-long scar on her neck, silver in the diffused light. "Who do you work for?"

"Xonex, the energy company."

He frowned. Xonex, the same company that had hired him for his expertise in handling situations exactly like this.

He frowned. It didn't add up. Why was she dressed in black, prowling around the deck in the early hours?

She was staring up at him, petrified. Her eyes, light-brown flecked with gold, were wide and frantic. Even terrified, there was something fierce, yet vulnerable about her. He eased off a little on her wrists, but not enough that she could wriggle free.

He had to be sure.

"You work here? On the *Explorer*?"

"That's what I've been telling you." Angry eyes glared at him, and she tossed some messy chocolate-brown strands out of her face.

"Then why are you dressed like a cat burglar?"

She spluttered. "Cat burglar? This is my yoga outfit."

"Yoga? You're kidding." Now he'd heard it all.

"I'm an engineer. I told you, I work here."

Confused, he stared at her, trying to get her measure. Lean and curved in all the right places, with cascades of deep brown hair framing a pale, pretty face, she didn't look anything like an engineer—then again, she didn't look like any intruder he'd ever encountered either. A yoga guru, yes. Ironically, that was the easiest to believe.

"Where is your ID?" he asked, his face so close he could breathe in her scent. Vanilla—warm, inviting, disarming.

She grimaced. "I–I left it in my room."

He sighed.

Really?

"You have no ID, but you expect me to believe you work here?"

"I do." She gave a sexy pout.

He narrowed his eyes. "How come I haven't seen you before?"

"I flew in yesterday evening. Actually, I saw you and your friend up on deck, but you didn't see me."

He frowned. He hadn't noticed her. Could be a convenient excuse. "What are you doing prowling around the deck at five in the morning?"

She wriggled again, her hips digging into his thighs. For a small woman, she was remarkably strong. He pressed down, then wished he hadn't. A surge of heat spread to his groin, which was still pulsing from connecting with her knee.

"Isn't it obvious? I'm doing yoga." Irritation replaced the fear. That was something, at least. He hadn't liked seeing how panicked she'd been.

He knew fear, and hers had been very real. Desperate, terrifying, irrational fear. Experience had taught him he wasn't the reason. Something else had caused that fear, something bad, and a while back. But she hadn't let it go.

"Yoga, right…" His voice petered off.

The way she was looking at him… all bristly and defiant, her tiger's eyes flashing in the hazy dawn. He wanted to believe her, but he had to check it out fully before he let her go.

She could just be a really good liar. The whole yoga thing

might be nothing but a smokescreen. For all he knew, an activist group had sent a bombshell like her to stir up trouble over the oil drilling.

This wasn't new territory for him. After a solid twenty years in the service, with a good chunk as a Navy SEAL, he was no stranger to diehards on a mission. People got pretty intense when they truly believed in a cause.

"Look, I just got here yesterday." She snapped, clearly ticked off. "If you get off me, I'll take you to my cabin and show you my ID badge. Then we can clear this whole mess up."

Now that was the first sensible thing he'd heard her say.

"Sounds like a plan." Letting go, he released her hands. He'd check her out, and if she was telling the truth... well, then he'd owe her an apology. Somehow, he didn't mind that too much.

She huffed. "Can I get up now?"

"All right, but just so we're clear, you're sticking with me until I know you're legit."

She gave a quick nod and another small exhale.

He backed off, then offered a hand up.

She ignored it, got to her feet, then brushed herself off, but not before throwing him a look that could melt steel.

"After you," he gestured, resisting a grin. She really was a hellcat.

She walked ahead of him along the narrow gangway, swishing her hips as she went. Groaning silently, he followed.

Was she toying with him? Trying to provoke him?

He followed that sexy ass down the corridor, trying to stay focused, but damn if she wasn't making it difficult. Inappropriate thoughts crept unbidden into his head, not helped by the memory of her flushed face, soft skin and sensual stride.

They reached the door that descended into the crew's quarters, and she glanced back—big eyes, asking permission, but not without a mocking glare.

He nodded and down they went, the greenish glow of emergency lights bathing everything in an eerie tint, the rig creaking around them. He had to admit, she seemed to know where she was going.

"My roommate is still sleeping." She hesitated outside one of the cabin doors.

"I'll wait here."

So, the little vixen had been telling the truth, but he had to play by the book. Everyone onboard had to wear their ID card. No exceptions.

She slipped into her room, leaving the door cracked just enough so he could glimpse inside. Last time he'd let his guard down, it had almost cost him. He wasn't about to make the same mistake twice. Women could be full of surprises.

Then she was back, dangling her ID right in his face. "Satisfied?"

Phoenix checked it out, squinting in the murky light.

Eleanor Rider, Chemical Engineer, Xonex Energy Services.

Okay, so she was on the level.

He handed it back to her, meeting her triumphant gaze. "Thank you, Eleanor Rider. Sorry about the inconvenience. I had to make sure, you understand. We take security very seriously on the *Explorer*."

He saw a flicker of fear return, but she covered it well. "I suppose you were just doing your job."

He gave a brusque nod. "Yes, ma'am."

She sniffed, not quite ready to forgive him. "You should think twice next time you jump a stranger." Her gaze roamed over his physique, and he thought he detected a reluctant flicker of appreciation. "A man your size, you could hurt somebody."

"In my line of work, a delay could mean loss of life." His eyes bore into hers. "Just remember to wear your ID in future. It will save further… misunderstandings."

She tossed the loose strands of hair over her shoulder as she spun around to go back inside the cabin. "Don't worry, I will."

CHAPTER 3

*T*hat man!

Ellie perched on the edge of her bed, buzzing with a weird kind of electric energy that left her both flustered and excited.

What the hell?

She didn't know what to make of him. He was certainly efficient, the way he barreled into her, sending her flying. And strong—that effortless force, biceps of steel. She had tried her hardest to throw him off, and since those self-defense classes, she was no pushover. Not anymore.

Yet, he hadn't so much as budged. Not even an inch. An immovable mountain of stone. A shiver shot threw her at the thought of him sitting on top of her. No way was that his full weight. He'd been holding back, she was sure of it. That made it even more incredible, that he'd rendered her helpless while not even using his full strength. She could only imagine what he'd do to a real intruder.

But why was she so strung out?

She knew why.

Rafael.

Damn him. Ever since the incident, she couldn't be in an even remotely threatening situation without feeling her heart leap and her palms go sweaty as her anxiety spiraled out of control. It had been that way for the last two years.

The security operative had only been doing his job. *She'd* been the one at fault, not wearing her ID badge.

Typical.

Henderson had warned her. Make sure you have it on you at all times, he'd said.

And what had she done?

The first instance she'd left the room, she'd damn well forgotten it. Simple protocol that she *knew* and still neglected. It must be the upheaval of the last few days. She blamed jetlag. Her head was all over the place, trying to figure out which time zone she was in.

Picking up the lanyard, she slung it over her head. The ID photograph on the front caught her eye. It wasn't her finest moment, but it wasn't bad. In her business suit, hair clipped up, a smattering of make-up, she looked like the seasoned professional she was.

Three years working for a petrochemical company in Saudi Arabia, then another two in Scotland. This wasn't her first time in the field, so she should be used to the protocols by now.

Sucking in a deep breath, she tried to calm down. Well, she wasn't about to let the Beast ruin her first day on the job. No, sir.

Looking around the room, she realized her yoga mat was still lying up on the helipad.

Crap.

Now she'd have to sneak back and get it. The last thing she wanted to do was run into the Beast again, but she couldn't leave it there. Once the chopper began transporting people to the rig, someone would remove it, then she'd have a hard time finding it and would probably get reprimanded for leaving it there. Worse, it could blow off and be gone forever.

Reluctantly, she got up, her body complaining at the sudden movement. Lifting her T-shirt, she inspected her bruised ribs. Great, just great. That was where he'd smashed into her. Her elbow stung too, where she'd scraped it on the deck when she'd fallen.

She sighed. No real harm done. It would heal in due course. Once, she'd tripped and fallen down a set of steel steps on the North Sea rig, and that had hurt a damn sight more.

Careful not to wake Suzi, Ellie opened the cabin door then ventured back topside. The sky was softening in the east, where a thin sliver of liquid sun was just poking its head over the very flat horizon.

It was stunning, and she gasped in delight. It had been a while since she'd seen a sunrise so breathtaking.

In Scotland, the sky had always been fifty shades of gray, and in the Middle East, the sun had seemed to pop up, already fully formed, a bright, burning fireball.

Pity to waste it. The deck was still quiet, with nobody on duty yet. The Beast was nowhere to be seen, and apart from the odd creak of machinery and the soft whistle of the warm breeze through the metal beams of the rig, it was just her and the sky and the vast ocean.

Perfect for a sun salutation.

This way she'd still get her routine in, albeit a shortened version. God knew she needed it, especially now with the bruises on her side and her stiffening elbow.

Yoga had always been her reset button. She'd taken it up after the incident with Rafael as a way to calm her anxiety, and it had worked. She didn't suffer nearly so much anymore.

It was only when something bad happened, like today, when she flipped, and it all came rushing back. She hadn't had a panic attack like this morning's for almost a year now.

The ocean had a calming effect. Feeling more composed, she stepped onto her mat then brought her hands together in the prayer position. Slowly, she lifted her arms upward, hands still together, stretching her body backward slightly, opening her chest and focusing on the stretch. *Breathe*, she heard her yoga instructor say.

She bent forward from the waist, trying to clear her mind, but like a tune that wouldn't go away, she kept seeing *him* sitting on top of her, his massive hand forcing hers above her head.

Her breath came faster, and she fought to still it. Placing her hands flat on her mat, she focused on the stretch in her back and legs and not on the probing look in his eyes that had burned into her.

It was insane how easily he'd overpowered her. Frightening, really. And after all the training she'd done to ensure that exact situation didn't happen again.

Okay, she was rattled. Well and truly freaked out. What had happened this morning was a reminder that no matter how strong she'd become, she was still weaker than a man.

Goddammit.

That annoyed her.

Inhaling more sharply than she wanted, she stepped her right leg back, dropping her knee to the floor, feeling the pull in her hip flexors.

The sky was a fading midnight blue, the exact hue of his eyes. Hissing out an annoyed breath, she extended her other leg and assumed the stick pose, bringing her body into a straight line.

For some reason, it was unusually hard to balance. Her

core stability was shot—and she knew exactly who to blame for that.

The sun rose above the horizon, and the the peachy-orange sky burst outward. Ellie reveled in the warmth on her face, as she lowered her body to a prone position. Soaking in the energy, she closed her eyes, pushed through her hands, and curved her spine.

Damn, this felt great.

Slowly, she was coming alive.

As she straightened her arms and legs to form an inverted V, the tension of the last few hours finally dissipated. The fear she'd been harboring began to subside, and her natural confidence came back.

It had been a case of mistaken identity. He'd thought she was an intruder, prowling around on deck dressed in black.

Who could blame him?

But it wouldn't happen again, not now he knew who she was.

Ellie went through the remainder of the yoga sequence, feeling herself grow stronger with every asana. Finally, when she brought her arms down and came to rest in the prayer position, she felt like a new woman.

Today was a fresh start, an opportunity to advance her career by leading a project she was passionate about. The *Explorer* would unearth test samples and she would analyze them and determine their viability. She was a strong, capable, independent woman.

She was not a victim.

As the sun rose higher and workers started appearing on deck, she picked up her mat and headed to her cabin. There was still plenty of time for a shower and breakfast in the cafeteria before starting her shift. It was going to be a good day.

. . .

ELLIE STARED at the data on the computer screen in front of her. Okay, maybe her earlier optimism had been slightly premature. She'd just run a test on the samples from the first site through the X-ray fluorescence analyzer, which gave her an idea of the quality and composition of the various elements within the samples.

Except it didn't contain what she was expecting.

Usually, in viable samples, she found light hydrocarbons, low contaminants, and a degree of rock permeability. All the geological surveys had pointed to that being true, but what she was seeing was the complete opposite.

Puzzled, she mulled over the results. It didn't add up. Was it possible they were drilling in the wrong place? Not likely. Had there been a mistake with the coordinates? That was possible, but it would be a very expensive error, if it was. And Suzi would have double-checked the survey reports before she input the coordinates into the system.

Ellie decided she'd check the geological report herself.

Getting up, she left her lab and headed to the control center. This was the hub of the rig from where the drilling operations were directed.

She rounded a corner and...

"Oomph!" The air wheezed out of her like a punctured balloon.

Reeling, she staggered backward, her legs flying out from under her. She put out an arm to steady herself, but instead of the cold wall encountered something almost as hard but much hotter.

His torso.

An arm shot out and hooked around her waist, preventing her from falling over. In one smooth movement, he lifted her up then deposited her back on her feet. It happened so fast, it made her head spin.

"Holy crap, it's you."

They were pinned together, her hands spread over his chest. She felt his muscles tense beneath her fingers, surprised by the heat it stirred.

A terse response. "It's me."

Those midnight blue slits glinted down at her, jolting her back to her senses. Unlike this morning, he wasn't dressed in combat gear but instead wore a pair of shorts and a casual T-shirt with a surfing logo on it. It made him look less severe, more carefree. She could almost picture him on a beach in Cali, a surfboard under his arm.

"We have to stop meeting like this," he said, dryly.

"Sorry." She lifted her hands off his chest. "I wasn't looking where I was going."

The glint changed to a concerned frown, and he gently released her. "Are you okay?"

"Yeah, I'm fine. Thank you," she added, as an afterthought, her face burning.

He fixed that unnerving blue gaze on her, and she was sure she saw a flicker of admiration. "I see you're calling the shots now."

"Huh?" She wasn't quite sure where he was going with this. In her head, she was still squished against him, feeling his body heat, his arms looped around her waist.

"Well, you rock up and the next day things start happening." He nodded toward the control room where a noisy hum sounded, accompanied by deep vibrations signaling drilling was in progress.

"They're drilling the fourth test well," she explained, looking down—anywhere but at him. If only the heat in her cheeks would calm down. "They're on a schedule, which doesn't have anything to do with me. I'm just here to analyze the samples."

That served as a reminder. She needed to get to the control center to take a look at those survey maps. "If you'll excuse me."

"Sure." He stepped aside, letting her pass. She caught a whiff of men's aftershave. Warm and spicy with a smokey hue that lingered after she'd passed by. Actually, it wasn't lingering, it was on her blouse.

Great.

It wasn't enough that he'd invaded her thoughts. Now she'd be smelling him for the rest of the day too.

CHAPTER 4

This job had been a lifeline. After what had happened in Basra, Phoenix couldn't face another tour with the SEALs. Not with *that* hanging over him.

Two men were dead because of him. Two good men.

His friends.

Phoenix sat staring into his plate of untouched food. The cafeteria actually dished up some decent grub, but he didn't have an appetite. All he could taste was guilt.

"Is it not good?" asked a feminine voice.

He glanced up to see Minnie, the Texan chef who made most of their meals, smiling blatantly down at him. She had big brown eyes, a mass of blonde curls, and a strong Texan drawl. The roughnecks who worked shifts on the rig often talked about her, and in ways that didn't always sit well with him.

"No, that's not it. It's great, really. I'm just not that hungry."

Her eyes flitted shamelessly over him. "A man like you needs to eat. It will keep you strong." She flexed her bicep, showing off long, tapered arms.

He forced a smile and picked up his knife and fork. Couldn't disappoint the chef. Minnie had been flirting with him since the day he arrived. It didn't bother him. In fact, he was used to it, and normally, he'd be up for a bit of fun, but since he'd left the Navy, he'd been stoically single.

He couldn't figure out if it was because he didn't feel worthy of having fun, not when he'd caused the death of two of his team, or if a no-strings one nighter had just lost its appeal in the wake of the far more serious issue he was dealing with. Whatever the reason, he wasn't ready for close human contact, which meant dating was out of the question.

He forced down a few mouthfuls, then looked up again as the hellcat, Eleanor Rider, walked in with her roommate, Suzi. He'd met Suzi a couple of times through Boomer, who he shared a room with, and liked her. She was bubbly and gregarious, a real breath of fresh air. Secretly, he thought Boomer was into her but was too shy to say anything.

Boomer, even though he had his fair share of women, wasn't known to make the first move. Luckily, being built like a machine, and with features women found attractive, he rarely had to.

"Hey, Phoenix." Suzi stopped at his table. He didn't miss Eleanor stiffen. "Want some company?"

"I won't be here long," he said, with an apologetic shrug. Everything in *her* body language indicated she'd rather not sit with him. "My shift starts in fifteen."

"That's okay, we don't mind." Suzi sat without being asked, and Phenix saw Eleanor give a little sigh. She wasn't alone in her reluctance. He wasn't in the mood for small talk either. He'd slept most of the morning after he'd bumped into her, catching up on the night before, and then spent the afternoon working out in the gym, venting some of the frustration he always seemed to carry around with him.

Usually, it helped, but today, for some reason, it had just made things worse.

Dressed in his operational clothes, he still had to go back to his cabin and put on his tactical vest and pick up the rest of his gear. There was a long night ahead.

Eleanor sat down, her leg brushing his under the table.

"Sorry," she mumbled.

He managed a small grin. "Did you get to where you were going in such a hurry earlier?" She'd been so preoccupied when they'd bumped into each other, it must have been somewhere important.

Her big brown eyes widened. "Oh, yes, thank you. I did."

"You two know each other?" Suzi asked, surprised.

"Not officially," Phoenix said. Intriguingly, Eleanor didn't appear so feisty now. This was a different side to her. He'd seen the hellcat and the thoughtful professional, but now she looked distracted, distant.

"Oh, well in that case, meet my new roomie, Eleanor. She's here for the duration of the project, so you'll be seeing her around quite a lot."

"Call me Ellie." The hellcat extended her hand.

Phoenix shook it, engulfing it with his big one. A vision of holding them above her head on the hard deck of the helipad only that morning flashed into his head.

That was the problem with oil rigs, he reasoned. The permanent staff were confined to small living spaces, so everyone got to know each other very well. Too well, in some cases.

"Ellie's a chemical engineer," Suzi added. "She's heading up the testing project."

"Really?" He couldn't help but be impressed. He'd thought operations had sped up since she'd arrived, but modestly, she'd played it down.

"Phoenix," he said, releasing her hand.

She put it back in her lap, her curious gaze still on his face. He noticed her brown eyes were shot through with yellow, making them look like they were glowing. "Phoenix. Like the bird that rose from the ashes?"

"Yeah. It's a nickname I was given in the Navy because I was always the last one standing. The phoenix apparently lived for five hundred years." Or so he'd been told.

How ironic that the prophecy had turned out to be true. He was still standing, where all the others had fallen, and now he had to deal with survivor's guilt.

That's what they called it—therapists, magazine articles, Google.

"You were in the Navy?" Her eyebrows rose.

"Yeah, but not anymore."

"Why's that?"

It was an innocent enough question, but one he wasn't prepared to answer. "It was time for a change."

There was an awkward pause.

"Boomer and Phoenix both work for the same private security company." Suzi said, effortlessly filling the gap. "What's it called again?"

"Blackthorn Security. It's run by a buddy of mine."

Truth be told, he'd been floating around doing nothing in particular, drinking too much and hanging out in pool bars, when Blade had approached him. Blade, also ex-military, had been medically discharged from the army shortly before Phoenix had bailed on the SEALs, and was now running operations for Blackthorn.

At first, Phoenix had said no, he wasn't up to it. His fitness had gone to shit, and he was still reeling from what had happened. Blade, who knew what it was like to be at a loose end, hadn't taken no for an answer. So, here he was.

But he didn't tell them any of that.

23

"Boomer was in explosives," Suzi continued, a note of pride in her voice.

Those two were definitely into each other. It was obvious just by watching how animated she became when she talked about him.

"He used to defuse bombs for a living. Can you imagine doing that?"

"I can't." Ellie shook her head. "It must have been very stressful."

"Yeah, that's why he left," Suzi said. "He had a close call and figured enough was enough."

Close call? That was one way of putting it.

Boomer had obviously given her the watered-down version. In reality, an IED had exploded while he was attempting to disarm it, and he'd gotten a lungful of shrapnel. It had taken six months, multiple surgeries, and weeks of rehab to remove it all and heal up. Afterwards, he'd decided not to go back to work, and Phoenix didn't blame him.

Being a U.S. Navy SEAL took its toll, and they all had scars to show, but he missed the camaraderie of the unit. He and his team had been in some real hell holes together over the years, but the bonds they'd forged were deep and abiding. That's why it hurt so goddamn much losing two of them.

He turned back to Ellie. "So what was the hurry this morning?"

She frowned, her forehead lining. "I analyzed the first few samples today, but they weren't what I was expecting. I thought we might have gotten the coordinates wrong, so I was on my way to check the geographical survey maps. That's when I bumped into you."

"But they were accurate," Suzi qualified, joining in.

Ellie nodded. "Yes, everything was correct, so it can't be that."

"What were you expecting?" Phoenix sensed there was

more to this problem than Ellie was letting on. He'd become experienced at reading people during his time in the SEALs —lives depended on making the right judgement call—and he could tell something was bothering her.

"A different composition of elements, that's all. Something more in-line with the satellite imaging that had been done." She waved a hand in the air. "It's not important. I'll retest tomorrow. It's probably just a problem with my samples."

She was making light of it, but he didn't push.

"Is your shift an all-nighter?" Suzi asked, and he got the feeling she was thinking about Boomer.

"2000 to 0800," he replied, catching Ellie's eye. Was she also thinking about their surprise meeting in the early hours of the morning?

What Ellie didn't know was he'd seen her come back and finish her yoga routine on the helipad. Keeping to the shadows—he hadn't wanted to interrupt her again—he'd watched as she'd worked through the various movements with a grace and fluidity he'd admired. Hell, he'd more than admired it. He couldn't keep his damn eyes off it.

"Do you switch to days next week?" Suzi asked, obviously wondering if she'd be able to hang out with Boomer more often.

After an answering nod, he stood. "I've got to head off. I'm due on shift."

"Have fun," Suzi said, cheerfully. "Say hi to Boomer for me."

"Will do." Phoenix turned to Ellie, a half-smile on his face. "Can I expect to see you on the helipad at five tomorrow?"

She turned pink and glared at him. Just like that, the hellcat was back. "Don't count on it."

He chuckled. "Pity."

She refused to look at him.

Smiling, and in a better mood than he had been in all day, he went back to his room to get kitted up.

* * *

"Okay, what's going on between you two?" Suzi blurted out the moment Phoenix had left the cafeteria.

Ellie turned away. "Nothing. What made you ask that?"

"Just the friggin' tension flying between you." She shook her head. "I mean, come on!"

"I don't know what you're talking about," Ellie mumbled. "Maybe we should eat?"

"Hang on a moment." Suzi's eyes twinkled. "You're not getting away that easy. What happened this morning? Come on, spill."

"It was just a little misunderstanding. I was doing yoga on the helipad, and he thought I was an intruder."

Suze gave a loud snort. "Seriously?"

"Yeah, he jumped me and pinned me down. Unfortunately, I didn't have my ID on me, so he didn't believe me when I told him who I was."

She guffawed. "Ellie, how could you forget your ID?"

"I know. It was totally my fault. I had to take him to our room to get it. Only then did he let me go."

Suzi giggled, a light airy sound.

It was contagious, and Ellie found herself smiling too. "I'm a little embarrassed."

"I wouldn't mind being jumped by the likes of him."

"It wasn't enjoyable at the time." Memories of her panic attack flooded back. "He gave me a hell of a fright."

"He is a trained killer," she said, with a touch of admiration. "He could probably crush you with his bare hands if he wanted to."

Now that was a comforting thought.

"I'm starving." Ellie'd had enough of talking about this topic and stood up. "We should have grabbed our food before sitting. Let's eat."

"Fine, but we're going to discuss this another time." Suzi joined her. "That man likes you, I can tell."

"Nonsense."

"So, are you going to see him tomorrow morning?" Suzi picked up a plate.

Ellie turned her back on her friend. "I don't know. I haven't decided yet." Morning yoga was something she really enjoyed. Despite what she'd said, she didn't want to give it up just because she was avoiding a certain beast of a man.

"If you enjoy it, you should go," Suzi said. "It's a big rig. You might not see him at all."

It wasn't that big.

Should she?

It would be a shame to miss it.

On the rig where there was little opportunity to exercise, she enjoyed the invigorating postures. It also kept her supple and relaxed her, mentally preparing her for the day.

"Yeah, I probably will." Decision made.

Ellie loaded up her plate with a hearty serving of brisket, fluffy cornbread, and a side of tangy coleslaw. After a decent meal and a good night's sleep, she'd be raring to go at the crack of dawn. More so than this morning, when she had still been groggy from the flight and the unfamiliar bed.

One thing was sure—her decision had absolutely nothing to do with a certain, brutally hot, security operative who would be patrolling the rig during the early hours.

Nothing at all.

CHAPTER 5

"*I* thought you weren't coming."

Ellie spun around at the deep, gravelly voice. Phoenix emerged from the shadows like a specter—so stealthy, she hadn't heard him coming.

"I decided I wanted to. It's a good routine to get into," she countered, then flushed. Was that too defensive? The last thing she wanted was to make him think she'd gotten up early to see him.

He gave her a strange look. "I just meant it's refreshing to see you. It's been a pretty boring night."

"That's a good thing, right?" she replied, after a moment's hesitation. He was just being friendly. She needed to lighten up.

He chuckled, his eyes sparkling in the predawn light. "In this job, definitely."

Ellie laid her mat on the ground and kicked off her shoes. As usual, the day was dawning clear and bright, the sky mostly cloudless indigo with a faint slash of pink over the horizon.

"Do you do yoga every morning?" He was staring at her

pink toenails. She'd had them done on a whim before leaving Scotland.

"If I can, but rigs don't often offer this kind of opportunity. The last one I worked on was operational 24/7, so I couldn't workout outside. It's just with all this beauty around me—" She waved her hand in the fresh morning air. "It would be a shame not to."

He stood, legs slightly apart, shoulders relaxed, holding his weapon in front of him, seemingly at ease. Ellie couldn't read the expression on his face, but it was almost like he was measuring her up. She'd love to know what he was thinking. Probably that a dirty rust-bucket in the middle of the ocean was no place for a woman. Well, if that's what he thought, then he could—

"Where'd you work before?"

His question surprised her. She was expecting a disparaging remark. This was when they usually said something like, *Do you enjoy working on oil rigs?* Or *It's a strange occupation for a girl.*

"North Sea. Clair Ridge, Platform 44." The words rolled off her tongue with pride.

His blue eyes widened. "North Sea. Wow. How long were you out there for?"

Okay, so maybe he wasn't thinking that. There was only admiration in his warm gaze. "Just over two years."

He whistled softly. "That's a long time. I knew a guy who worked out there. He said the money was good, but the weather was goddamn awful." He glanced out at the dark blue expanse of ocean. "I'd take a pay cut for this any day."

He had a faraway look in his eye, like he was someplace else. She followed his gaze, enjoying the gentle breeze on her face. "Can't argue with that." As the seconds ticked by, she realized she knew very little about him. "Where were you before?"

He hesitated, then dragged his gaze back to her. "My last op was in Afghanistan."

She nodded. "I worked in Saudi Arabia for a while, before the North Sea assignment. It was my first job after college."

His eyes narrowed, almost wistfully. "I never got used to the sun over there. Big blazing ball of fire in the sky. In summer, the heat was pretty relentless."

"I remember." It had been the same where she had worked at the oil field. "Thank God everywhere had AC."

He snorted. "Not where I was. Dehydration was a real threat."

She could imagine. "Do you miss it?"

He started. "Why'd you ask that?"

She shrugged. "Just an impression I got listening to you talk about it, that's all."

His shoulders slumped. "I don't miss it, although I do miss my buddies."

She knew what that was like. "I'm sure. I miss my friends on the 44, too."

He tilted his head and studied her. Ellie felt a surprise flutter in her stomach. What the hell? She didn't normally go for this type of guy. Base, brute strength and brawn. When she thought about settling down one day, it was usually with a scientist, a professor of geology or an engineer. Someone with shared interests and a dazzling intellect.

Not someone like… *him*.

Then she got it. It was so much that she was attracted to Phoenix as he intrigued her—and she'd always loved a good mystery. Whether it was analyzing samples to see what secrets they held or doing a crossword puzzle on a rainy day, she liked to solve things. Even as a kid she'd enjoyed breaking stuff down into its core parts to see what it was made of.

"I guess you know what it's like, then."

"Huh?"

"Missing your friends." He gave her a quizzical look.

"Oh, yeah." She nodded, silently chastising herself for losing concentration.

A pause stretched between them.

Eventually, he said, "Well, duty calls. I've got to continue with my rounds. Catch you later."

"Yeah. See ya."

He gave a quick nod then disappeared around the corner of the rig into the predawn shadows.

* * *

PHOENIX SAT IN THE CAFETERIA, coffee in hand, flipping through a discarded issue of *Oil & Gas Magazine*. He sensed Ellie walk in before he saw her. Looking up, he noticed she was alone, and by the expression on her face, deep in thought. Eyes fixed on the ground, she nearly bumped straight into another worker.

"Oh, I'm sorry," she said, without glancing up. He watched as she wove around more people then sat on one of the armchairs near the coffee station to the side of the main dining area.

She didn't get a beverage, nor did she look up. She simply sat there, staring out of the smudgy window in front of her at the blurry expanse of blue ocean, a confused expression on her face.

Wondering if he was doing the right thing, Phoenix rose and went over. She glanced up as he eased his frame into the vacant armchair beside her. "Something wrong?"

"Oh, hi. I didn't realize you were here."

"I know. You were miles away."

A self-conscious laugh. "Yeah, I'm trying to figure something out, and to be honest, I'm finding it pretty tough."

"Anything I can help with?"

A wry smile played at her lips. "That's kind of you, but I don't think so."

"Why? Because I wouldn't understand?" He bit out the words without thinking. Damn it. He hadn't meant to sound so cutting, especially not when he was trying to help.

Her eyebrows rose. "Are you a chemist?"

"No, but that doesn't mean I won't be able to help in some other way."

She stared at him a long moment, then gave a nod. "Okay, fine."

He held up a finger. "Wait. Let me get you some coffee first, then you can tell me, and I'll see if I can offer any assistance."

She laughed, her shoulders relaxing. "Okay, deal."

He went over to the machine, fixed her a cup just how he figured she'd like it—no sugar, straightforward, like her. Handing her the cup, he watched as she took an absent-minded sip. It must be okay, as she didn't complain, simply nodded her thanks.

"Okay, what's up?" he prodded, sitting down again.

She wrapped her hands around the mug, as if she needed the comfort it gave her. Those small hands, elegant and lady-like. "I've now analyzed the samples from all three test sites, and there is no evidence of hydrocarbons. Nothing. But according to the geological reports, there should be."

She was right. He knew nothing about oil reservoirs, but it might help her to talk it out. "These are the geological reports you were looking at the other day?"

She nodded.

"What are the reports based on?"

"Seismic reflection imaging, mostly."

Was his expression as blank as his mind at that moment?

Must have been, as she offered a brief smile with an explanation.

"The geological survey company bounces sound waves through the rock surface and captures the echoes with sensors. The different angles provide a picture from beneath the surface of the site being surveying."

"And that pinpoints where the oil is?"

"Sort of. We then run the data through high-performance computers using complicated algorithms to produce a geological map. That gives us images we can interpret and analyze." She smiled self-consciously. "I sound like a complete geek, huh?"

"No. I actually understood that," he said with a self-conscious chuckle. He must be nuts if he thought he had anything in common with this woman. She was smart, sassy, and driven. She solved the earth's deepest mysteries while he… he was built for battle, not brains.

"Suzi's looked at them too," she continued, oblivious to his self-deprecating thoughts, "and we're in agreement. The reservoirs are beneath us, but we're not finding anything but rock, sand, and seawater."

Phoenix thought about this. "What does Henderson say?"

"That's the strange thing. He doesn't seem concerned. I told him we should have found evidence of oil by now, but he just told me to keep trying. That we'll find it in one of the samples."

"Maybe he's right. Could be you're worrying for nothing."

She frowned. "Maybe. But one of the samples isn't enough. It won't be economically viable. I was expecting to get results from *all* the test samples. I'll try again tomorrow. The company is employing me to get results. I'll just have to keep digging until I find something."

He gave an uncertain nod. He might not know the first

thing about seismic surveys or oil reservoirs, but he knew about duty and dedication—and Ellie had those in spades.

She bit her lip. "I'm sorry. Here I am waffling on about my work problems. How was your day?"

"Uneventful. I slept most of the morning, then worked out in the gym. You know how it is."

She gave an understanding nod. There were only so many things you could do on the rig in your down time.

"What made you go into private security?" she asked, and he knew she was just being polite and making conversation.

He shrugged. "Seemed like a good idea at the time."

"You don't like talking about yourself much, do you?" The way she was staring at him seemed like she had him pegged. Maybe she did.

He masked a grin. "Occupational hazard. I was in the Navy for nearly twenty years. Uncle Sam doesn't like us talking about operational stuff, so we learn to keep our mouths shut."

She nodded. "I get that. It's the same in my industry, but not because we can't talk about our work—although sometimes we can't. It's more because nobody else understands what we're talking about." Her lips curled.

He tried not to notice how enticing they were.

"Chemical engineering isn't the most exciting job in the world. Not like what you do."

"Private security can be pretty boring too," he said, thinking about last night, patrolling around the deserted rig, staring at nothing by blackness.

"I guess so, but you've seen your share of action. I can tell by the way you don't want to talk about it. We always avoid subjects we don't want to talk about."

He stared at her, long and hard. What was she? A shrink too? "What do you know about that?

She shrugged, and he recalled the look in her eyes when

he'd had her pinned to the ground the day before. Fear and panic, followed by a frenzied determination to throw him off. Anger, when she couldn't.

He'd been right. She'd experienced a traumatic event herself. One that she couldn't forget—or talk about.

"I know more than you think," she said softly, confirming his thoughts.

He detected a hint of sadness. As he knew very well, it was impossible to turn back time. How often had he wished that very thing? To go back to that day in Basra, to have that moment again.

The problem was, orders were orders. Truth be told, he'd have to make the same decision. The one that condemned his friends to a certain death.

Fuck.

It was on the tip of his tongue to ask her what it was that she couldn't let go of, but he didn't. Not because he didn't want to know—he was definitely curious—but because he wasn't sure he should. It was too easy talking to her. Getting personal meant crossing a line, and crossing lines led to other things like sharing confidences. Give and take. He'd have to reciprocate, and he couldn't do that.

Not yet.

Not to anyone.

Not even to a beautiful engineer who, under normal circumstances, he wouldn't mind getting to know.

Phoenix cleared his throat ignoring the pang of regret. As much as he wanted to confide in her, he couldn't. He was a mess—his head was all over the place. Opening up to her would just mean adding to that mess.

Besides, she was way out of his league. He'd just be opening himself up for disappointment. That was why he'd walked away that morning too. Made some dumb excuse about carrying on with his rounds. He could have spared a few more moments talking with her. Hell, with Boomer on the other side of the rig, he could have spared another hour, but he'd bailed.

Why?

The little voice that said he wasn't worthy. And it was shouting at him now.

He stood. "I've gotta get ready."

Ellie gave a little nod. "Thanks for the coffee—and for listening."

"I thought maybe if you got it off your chest, it would help a little."

"It did." She smiled, melting his heart just a little.

"See ya, Ellie."

"Bye, Phoenix."

He walked away, feeling her amber gaze burning a hole in his back.

CHAPTER 6

"*T*here's nothing wrong with the survey maps." Suzi scratched her head. "I've checked them multiple times. According to the geographical satellite images, you're absolutely right, we should find evidence of hydrocarbons and the correct composition of elements in the test samples."

"And yet I haven't." Ellie shook her head. "It doesn't make sense. Something's off."

"Henderson's instructions are to keep testing. Test everything that comes up, and if at the end of the six-month trial, we haven't found anything, the project will be shut down."

Ellie didn't point out what a monumental loss of investment that would be, a waste of millions of dollars in resources, an unnecessary environmental impact, not to mention downright puzzling, since according to all the survey data they had, they should be finding oil here.

On top of that, it would mean she'd failed. Her first solo engineer position, and she'd found nothing.

"There's nothing more you can do." Suzi rose to grab another soda. "Your job is to analyze the samples, that's it."

"I just hate not knowing why." She folded her arms across

her chest and stared unseeing at the wall-mounted television screen that—despite an old-style jukebox standing in the corner—played old music videos. The crew hung out and let off steam in this, the only recreational lounge on the rig. In addition to the two media sources, the room boasted a pool table, ping-pong table, and bar that only sold soft drinks.

"Above our pay grade," Suzi said. "You want one?"

She shook her head. "Nah, I think I'm going to get an early night. The jetlag is killing me." She hadn't been able to shake it off. Besides, she wasn't in the mood to have fun. The issue with the samples was driving her crazy. It was a puzzle she couldn't solve, and she wouldn't be able to let it go until she had answers.

"I've heard jetlag takes at least a week," Suzi said.

"I'll catch you later." Ellie pushed to her feet then turned to leave the hall.

FIVE A.M. and the deck was deserted.

"Looks like we're in for some weather," Phoenix's growly whisper came from directly behind her, making her jump. Still groggy from an interrupted night's sleep, her head hadn't woken up yet. He was seriously the stealthiest person she knew.

"I wish you'd stop doing that," she complained, hugging herself to ward off the chill. She'd underestimated the early morning temperature and had worn nothing but a tight, white T-shirt with her leggings—a choice she was deeply regretting.

His gaze dropped to her breasts, and blushing, she moved her arms across her erect nipples.

"You're cold."

No shit.

Before she had time to reply, he'd put down his rifle,

whipped off his tactical vest, and removed his sweatshirt, displaying through a tight tee a dazzlingly toned stomach with six-pack abs.

Holy hell. Did real men actually have bodies like that? He looked like he belonged on the cover of *Men's Health* magazine.

"Here, take this," he offered, the fabric still holding the heat of his body as he handed it to her.

She hesitated, but then tore her gaze away from his abdominals and pulled the sweatshirt over her head. It was like being enveloped in a part of him—his scent, warm and inviting, was a comforting contrast to the briny sea air. "Thank you."

"It looks good on you." He smiled in that secretive way. She noticed he had his vest back on, and his rifle was back in his hands. He'd managed all that while she'd been pulling on his shirt.

"Won't you be cold now?" His T-shirt strained around his biceps. Not that she minded the eye candy, but it didn't offer much in the way of warmth.

He shrugged. "Nah, I'm used to it. Besides, I'm going off duty in a couple of hours. I'll be fine."

There was a brief pause. The tension in the air wasn't just from the incoming pressure system. She was wearing his sweatshirt. It felt like him, smelled like him. Even though there was nothing between them, she couldn't get rid of the sensation of being covered by him.

Lord have mercy.

"This storm could delay the drilling," she ventured, grasping for a professional anchor. What the hell was wrong with her? Any longer and she was going to melt under that midnight-blue stare.

"Yeah, it'll rough up the seas. We're going to secure the

equipment and make sure everything's locked down. Best to stay below deck when it hits."

"We can monitor the weather system from the control deck," she said, unnecessarily. He didn't need to know that. She was babbling. Did he have any idea the turmoil her jetlagged brain was in?

"We'll check the rig's stabilizers, make sure everything's battened down," he added matter-of-factly. "There's no need to worry." She wasn't worried, she just wished he wouldn't look at her that way, like she was something he had to protect. No one had looked at her that way in a long time. She'd forgotten what it was like.

And if her stomach would just stop fluttering, she'd be able to think straight. "When is landfall? I mean, when is it going to hit us?"

"Within the next twenty-four hours," he confirmed. "It's due to hit the Florida coastline at 0200 hours, so I'd estimate an hour after that. It moves pretty quick."

"We've got some time to finish drilling on the fourth test site, then?"

He frowned. "How long will you need?"

"Another eight hours, give or take. According to Billy, the Operations Manager, we're nearly there—then we can start collecting samples."

"Eight hours is pushing it," he said. "I'd advise him to shut down operations by 1700 this afternoon, so we have time to make sure everything's secure before the storm hits."

Fair enough. Personnel safety was more important than her test samples. "I'll talk to him."

He gave a quick nod. "Feeling better now?"

Were her nipples still misbehaving? Heck, yeah, but she suspected that was more to do with him than the cold.

"I am, thank you." She could smell his aftershave on the sweatshirt, toying with her senses. It was like having him on top of her again, but instead of his hands holding her down, they were enveloping her.

Suddenly, she craved that. He was still giving off that hot, protective vibe, his clear blue eyes caressing her with their directness. Her gaze dropped to his lips—she couldn't help it—and before she knew it, he'd taken a step toward her.

A large hand reached out and wrapped around her waist, pulling her toward him. Her heart throbbed manically. It was terrifying… but at the same time, exhilarating.

This isn't me, a voice screamed inside her head, but she wasn't listening. A deep, primal urge had taken over. It consumed her, drawing her to him like a magnet. She wanted to feel his arms around her for real.

A strong gust of wind pummeled her, pushing her toward him, until she was so close she could feel the heat emanating from his body. Phoenix stared down at her, his expression tense, like he was trying to fight this attraction, or whatever it was between them, and failing.

She wasn't even trying to fight it.

He looped his other arm around her waist, locking her against him. Those rock-hard abs dug into her stomach, and her breasts pushed up against his chest.

Dear God.

She clung onto him, her legs suddenly wobbly, hearing a soft groan in the back of his throat as she did so. "Ellie."

Damn, he was easy to look at with his glittering blue eyes that softened when he looked at her, and that stubbly jaw that made her want to reach out and touch it. Her heart was pounding like a drill bit. Could he hear it?

Slowly, he lowered his head. It was going to happen. Right here, on the deck. He was going to kiss her… but then a dark shape appeared from behind the rigging.

"Everything all right here?"

Ellie gasped and pulled away. It was his friend, the other security operative.

"Holy shit, Boomer," Phoenix exploded, spinning around. "A little warning next time."

This guy was as stealthy as Phoenix was. If only her heart would stop pounding…

She stared at the good-looking man, in identical black clothing, a similar gun, but where Phoenix had longer, wayward hair, this guy had a short, military-style brush cut. This must be the guy Suzi was into.

"Was wondering where you'd gotten to, buddy." Boomer's his lips curled up in a grin.

"I'm right here." Phoenix shot him a withering glare.

Boomer laughed, a deep rumbling sound. Ellie could see why Suzi liked him. He had a kind, craggy face, with deep set eyes and a wide, warm smile. His arms were also thick and muscly, like Phoenix's, and his shoulders were almost as broad.

"You must be Suzi's roommate," Boomer said, extending a hand. "She's told me about you."

Ellie forced a smile, her legs still a little unsteady. "Likewise. Good to meet you, Boomer."

"Glad to see you're being looked after." He nodded to the black sweatshirt she was wearing.

Immediately, she flushed. "Yes, I stupidly underestimated how cold it was up here."

"Storm's coming." He echoed Phoenix's warning.

"Yes, and you know what, I'd better head back down." Her time was up, and she had to get ready for work, and then go and speak to Billy.

"Thanks for the shirt," she added.

Phoenix nodded. "No worries."

Another gust made her take a hurried step forward. It was

getting windy up here. She wasn't sure it was safe to keep drilling, even for half a day, let alone eight hours.

"Nice to meet you, Ellie," Boomer called as he strolled off to check on a rattling chain.

"I, um… I'd better go," she said to Phoenix.

He nodded, not quite meeting her eye. "Yeah, see you later."

She picked up her mat then hurried back toward the staircase. Before she descended, she glanced back. Phoenix stood staring after her, and his intense expression made her catch her breath. Then, before she could decide what to do about it, he turned his back and walked away.

CHAPTER 7

*E*llie had just entered the cafeteria in search of supper, after getting an update from the site supervisor, when she heard her name called.

"Ellie, over here!"

Looking up, her stomach tightened. Suzi was sitting with both Phoenix and Boomer, the guy who had interrupted their almost-kiss—or whatever that was—earlier that morning. Thankfully, the rush to finish drilling before the storm hit had occupied her thoughts all day, so she hadn't had time to analyze it.

A moment of madness, that's all it was. The dark... the cold... his sweatshirt. Nothing more.

Then she remembered the heat in his gaze as he'd pulled her toward him, and the deafening hammering of her heart as she'd moved into his arms—kinda like what it was doing now.

It had felt so easy, so natural—almost like she'd been on autopilot.

Then came that haunted expression, almost like he'd been in pain.

But why? She'd felt the tension in his arms as he'd put his hands around her waist and pulled her close. Heard the desperation in his tone when he'd groaned her name.

She had *not* imagined that. He'd been as attracted to her as she was to him, she was sure of it.

Now, here he was, lounging in his plastic molded chair, all brooding charm—jaw locked, shoulders stiff, and eyes narrowed into blue slits as he looked at her. She glanced around for an escape, but there was nowhere to go. Suzi was beckoning, and both men were watching her. To leave now would make the situation even worse.

So she took a deep breath and walked across the room, cheeks blazing. Upon reaching them, she forced a smile. "Hey."

"Look who I found lurking around the cafeteria." Suzi beamed at the two muscular men at her table. She looked extremely proud of herself. "Ellie, this is Boomer."

"We've met." Boomer winked at her. Under the bright fluorescent lights in the cafeteria, she saw he had the same self-confident machismo that seemed to be a prerequisite for military types. Big and brawny. His nose had been broken, likely several times and he had friendly, drooping eyes. Definite sex appeal.

"How are you guys?" She smoothed a hand over her hair, conscious that it must look like a bird's nest thanks to the gale force winds up on deck.

"Great," Boomer replied.

Phoenix merely grunted, clearly not in a good mood. Well, that made two of them.

"I'm always one step behind," Suzi groaned, glancing between the two of them.

"We met on deck this morning," Ellie said quickly. "Just as the storm was coming in."

"Yoga?" Suzi asked.

Ellie nodded. Not that she'd managed to do any, but Suzi seemed satisfied.

"How'd it go today?" Phoenix asked, surprising her with the question. "Did they finish drilling?"

"Yeah, they did." She was impressed he'd remembered. "Just in the nick of time. When the storm is over, we can collect the fourth set of samples."

"Hopefully with better results."

She pursed her lips. He *had* been listening.

"It's getting pretty hairy out there," Suzi said as the rain hurled itself against the Perspex, making it rattle.

"I know, I've just spoken to Billy."

"You shouldn't be topside," barked Phoenix, his forehead furrowed. "It's not safe."

Ellie was surprised by his terse tone.

"We've issued a warning for everyone to stay below deck until the worst is over," Boomer explained. As security operatives, they advised Henderson on safety procedures.

She nodded. "I won't go back up until the storm's over."

"I contacted the company that drew up the survey reports." Suzi said, changing the subject. "They're called Geo Services Limited, and they're based out of Houston."

Ellie shook her head, puzzled. "I've never heard of them."

"Me neither, but they're a reputable organization and do a lot of work in the Gulf of Mexico."

"Do you have a contact?" She studiously avoiding Phoenix's gaze. "Have you spoken to them?"

"Not yet. As soon as I do, I'll let you know."

"Are you eating?" Boomer asked. "The food is pretty good. Minnie is a local Texan chef, and she's in charge of lunch service today."

Ellie wasn't hungry, but she knew Boomer was right. She had to keep her energy levels up or she'd feel even worse. She got herself a tray and was served a big plate of chili con carne by a sexy blonde with huge eyes and a wide smile. Her name tag said Minnie.

Ellie didn't miss the lingering glance the chef cast in Phoenix's direction. Returning to the table, she ignored the odd tightening in her chest. Seemed she wasn't the only one who found the hulking operative attractive.

She sighed and sat down. Why did she even care? A man like Phoenix could have his pick of women. He was so not her type, so why had she nearly kissed him?

After their almost-kiss, she'd returned to her room, showered, then gotten ready for work. His sweatshirt still lay on her bed, untouched, like she was too scared to pick it up. Afraid it still had some sort of magic hold over her.

It was ridiculous, she knew that. Yet, being surrounded by his heat, his smell… it had affected her in a way she'd never imagined.

"How long is the storm supposed to last?" Suzi asked.

"A day, maybe two." Phoenix looked at Boomer for confirmation, and he nodded.

Ellie picked up her cutlery and was about to start eating when an almighty crash came from somewhere above them.

"Shit, what was that?" Suzi's eyes were wide.

Both Phoenix and Boomer were already out of their seats and running toward the door.

"Sounds like part of the rigging," Ellie gasped.

If it was, this was bad. Really bad.

Suzi jumped up and dashed after them. Ellie followed, as did several other rig workers and operating staff. The first person she saw once she got topside was a windswept Billy, the Operations Manager, yelling into a hand-held radio. "Get up here! We need to secure it."

"What was that??" she asked, looking around.

His face was grim as he held the radio away from his ear. "The crane. It fell over and crashed through the railing."

Rain lashed across the deck and tore at the rigging. The huge crash had been made by a mini crane that had toppled sideways onto the upper deck. The weight of it had buckled the side railing, which hung off the edge of the platform, banging against the metal structure. One of the steel bars had come loose and flapped around dangerously.

"It's going to fly off," Suzi yelled behind her. "It could hit someone."

Ellie grabbed a length of rope out of a nearby crate where they stored such items and ran over to the railing. "We can secure it with this."

The wind howled around her, threatening to blow her off the edge of the platform into the tumultuous seas below.

"Get back!" Billy shouted, running over. He took the rope from her hand. "Let me."

Suddenly, a piece of debris flew across the deck, smashed into the ops manager, and sent him careening backwards.

"Billy!" Ellie screamed. She dove for him but missed, and he fell over the edge, out of sight.

"Man overboard!" she screamed, clinging onto the broken railing. The wind buffeted perilously around her, the force so strong she could barely hang on.

"Help!" Suzi turned to where Phoenix and Boomer were working to secure the damaged crane. "Billy's fallen off the rig!"

CHAPTER 8

*P*hoenix saw Ellie hanging onto the broken railing, the wind threatening to tear her away and send her hurtling over the edge, and his heart nearly stopped.

Fuck, no!

The thought of losing her to the heaving ocean below was too horrifying to even contemplate.

"Hurry!" screamed Suzi, pointing down into the frantic swells. "Billy's down there and Ellie's in trouble."

"Go! We've got this," Boomer yelled as several roughnecks appeared to help him secure the crane.

Phoenix raced across the slippery deck, his brain already assessing the situation. It was nearly 1800 hours, and the storm was intensifying by the minute. Massive waves pounded the rig, sending sheets of spray into the air. The wind howled like a wild beast, tugging his clothes and making it hard to keep his balance. The last known position of the man overboard was directly below Ellie.

He grabbed a lifebuoy, fitted with a personal locator beacon, and sprinted to where she lay, clutching the railing.

He saw her hold was firm, and she wasn't in immediate danger.

Thank God.

"Billy fell," she sobbed. "He was trying to help me."

"Do you have eyes on him?" Phoenix yelled over the roar of the tempest. Now he knew she was safe he could concentrate on the missing man.

She shook her head, her face a mask of anguish. "No, but he went in right here."

Phoenix peered into the surging waves, straining to see through the driving rain. For a heart-stopping moment, there was nothing but frothing darkness. Then—there! A thrashing figure in the maelstrom.

"Got him!" He threw the lifebuoy toward the struggling form, praying the man could reach it.

Images of the two men he'd lost in Afghanistan flashed through his mind, their faces twisted in confusion and betrayal as they realized what he'd done. That he'd sacrificed them to save the others. Bile rose in his throat, and he swallowed hard, trying to focus on the present. This wasn't Basra.

Shaking off the ghosts of his past, he grabbed Ellie and hauled her to safety, away from the treacherous edge.

"Get below deck," he told her, his voice brooking no argument. "I'll save Billy."

She stared at him with huge, haunted eyes, hair hanging in dripping tendrils around her pale face. "You can't take the boat out in this. It's suicide!"

"It's all right." He gripped her shoulders. "I've done this before. I have to try."

"You have?" Her voice was small, almost lost in the howling gale.

"Navy, remember?"

She gave a worried nod.

"I need you to get me that weather data you told me you had access to. Can you do that?"

She inhaled sharply and nodded, a flicker of determination pushing back the fear in her eyes. "I can access the rig's meteorological subsystem. Sea currents, wind conditions, everything you need."

"Do it!" He thrust a radio into her trembling hand. "Use this to update me. And Ellie?" He waited until she met his gaze. "I will bring him back."

She gave another jerky nod and disappeared down the stairs, clutching the radio like a lifeline.

Phoenix turned to Boomer. "I need your radio, and I need the inflatable in the water, stat."

Boomer, who had finished securing the broken crane, handed over his radio without hesitation. He knew the drill, they'd gone through it countless times in their SEAL training. Wordlessly, they began prepping the inflatable for launch, working with the speed and precision that only came from years of experience in life-and-death situations.

It was a battle to lower the inflatable into the seething ocean. The little boat would be tossed about like a leaf in the maelstrom the moment it touched the water. Gritting his teeth, Phoenix jumped down into it, nearly losing his footing on the slippery floor. Boomer followed a second later, his face grim as he took the controls and fired up the engine.

The inflatable bucked and heaved as they powered out into the frothing darkness, leaving the looming shadow of the rig behind. Phoenix clutched the radio and the receiver for the locator beacon, his knuckles white. "Ellie, I need that data!"

Her voice crackled over the radio, barely audible over the shrieking wind. "Current coordinates are 32.7 degrees North, 119.8 degrees west. Sea currents moving northeast at 2 knots. Wind from the southwest at 50 knots, gusting to 70."

Phoenix relayed the information to Boomer, yelling to be heard over the storm. "Wind direction is at odds with the sea currents! Factoring in their influence, I think he's drifting north-northeast!"

Boomer nodded grimly and adjusted their course, piloting the little boat over the mountainous swells with white-knuckled control.

The receiver in Phoenix's hand crackled and beeped, the sound barely audible over the roar of the wind and waves. He stared at it in disbelief for a second, hardly daring to hope. The locator beacon!

"I've got a signal!" he shouted, squinting at the screen. "Bearing 025, range 200 meters!"

"Roger that," Boomer acknowledged, steering the inflatable in the indicated direction. Phoenix kept his eyes glued to the receiver, terrified the signal would disappear and they'd lose the beacon—and Billy—in the vastness of the enraged sea.

The receiver flickered, and the signal wobbled. Phoenix's heart leaped into his throat. "Come on, come on," he muttered under his breath, willing the signal to hold. Seconds stretched into eternity as he stared at the screen, the wind and rain lashing his face.

Then, just as he thought it was lost, the signal strengthened again. "There!" Phoenix pointed at a patch of turbulent water ahead. "Slow down!"

Boomer eased off the throttle. The inflatable crawled over the waves, wallowed in the troughs. Phoenix stood, heart pounding, as he scanned the heaving surface.

There, in the beam of their searchlight, a figure clung weakly to a lifebuoy, battered by the churning sea. Relief surged through him, followed instantly by a fresh jolt of fear. Getting to Billy would be one thing, getting him safely back to the rig would be another.

"Hang on, we're coming!"

They pulled alongside Billy's struggling form. Phoenix leaned precariously over the water, arm outstretched. For a terrifying second, he thought he wouldn't reach him, and the sea would claim the struggling man before he was hauled to safety. Then he grasped Billy's jacket. Heaving with all his strength, he dragged the spluttering, half-drowned man into the inflatable.

Billy collapsed on the deck, retching up seawater, his skin ghostly pale under the stark beam of the searchlight. Phoenix crouched down next to him, checking him over with shaking hands. The man was breathing but shivering violently, his lips tinged blue with cold. A livid bruise stood out on his temple where he must have struck something during his fall.

"Billy? Can you hear me?" Phoenix had to shout over the storm.

Billy's eyes fluttered open, unfocused. "C-Cold," he managed through chattering teeth.

Phoenix exhaled a shaky breath, relief and exhaustion hitting him like a physical blow. "Just hang in there, okay? We're going to get you back to the rig, get you warmed up. You're going to be fine." He reached for the survival blanket stowed under the inflatable's bench then tucked it around Billy's shivering form, trying to still the violent trembling.

He looked up at Boomer. "Let's get the hell out of here."

Boomer nodded, his face drawn and exhausted. He turned the inflatable in a wide circle, aiming the bow back toward the looming shape of the rig.

The journey back was a nightmare. The little boat struggled against the massive swells, and seawater slopped over its sides. Phoenix crouched over Billy's prone form, shielding him from the worst of it.

After what seemed an eternity, the rig loomed before them, a fortress of steel battered by the wind and waves.

As they drew near the launch zone, Phoenix and Boomer observed two figures bracing against the elements, waiting to assist. Together they tethered the inflatable to the hoisting straps and signaled the crane operator to commence the lift. Gradually, the vessel ascended toward the platform, laboring against the howling winds. The boat heaved and pitched as it was pummeled by the relentless storm.

"How is he?" Henderson asked, once they got to the top and the boat had been secured in the bay.

"He's alive," Phoenix reassured him as they transferred Billy's shivering form to the main deck. "But he needs medical attention."

"Help me take him to the clinic," Henderson ordered, as two other men came to help. "Good job, guys."

Phoenix looked out at the storm-wracked night, the wind howling like a wounded beast.

It was far from over.

The storm was intensifying, the worst yet to come. But for now, they were all safe. That was the main thing.

Phoenix straightened, wincing as his abused muscles protested. He met Boomer's eyes, saw his own exhaustion and grim determination reflected there. "We did it, brother. We got him."

Boomer gave a relieved nod, then raised his voice over the screaming wind. "Let's get under cover."

Together, they secured the inflatable and retreated below deck to wait out the worst of the storm.

CHAPTER 9

*E*llie stared at the dripping figures of Phoenix and Boomer, who'd handed a trembling Billy over to the medical team. "How did you find him?" she asked.

"There was a beacon on the buoy," Phoenix replied, wiping his face with a towel.

"Nothing we haven't done before," Boomer said modestly.

She frowned. "You rescue a lot of people in the Navy?"

Boomer glanced at Phoenix.

"Actually, we were Navy SEALs," Phoenix explained.

Ellie knew the SEALs were one of the most elite special operations forces in the world, but she didn't know much beyond what she'd seen in the movies or read in books. Of course, they'd be tough, highly trained, and capable of handling just about anything, but the specifics of what they did were a mystery to her.

Still, she couldn't help but feel a sense of awe as she looked at Phoenix and Boomer, realizing they had once been part of this specialist group. The thought of the dangerous missions they must have undertaken and the incredible challenges they had faced was enough to make her break out in a cold sweat. She panicked at the mere thought of violence. How ridiculous that would sound to them.

It was no wonder they had been able to locate and rescue Billy with such efficiency and composure. It all made sense now. The way they carried themselves—the quiet confidence, the physical strength, and the unwavering focus.

Navy SEALs.

There was that fluttering in her chest again. After what she'd been through with Rafe, that protect and serve mentality was incredibly appealing.

This guy risked his life to save others and was still doing it even though he'd left the Navy.

"How are you doing?" Phoenix asked.

"Me? I'm fine. I wasn't the one thrown in the Gulf. Or the ones saving him," she replied, touched by his concern. Even though she felt wrung out, her entire body drained of adrenaline, weak and shaky, she was a hell of a lot better than Billy.

"I know, but you nearly went in. What happened?"

"The railing was broken. Suzi and I were trying to tie it down. We were worried it would break loose and hit someone in the storm. Then Billy shouted for me to get back. He pushed me out of the way, just before that thing came out of nowhere and hit him."

"What thing?" Phoenix asked.

"I don't know what it was. A piece of debris or part of the rigging. It had obviously come loose and turned into a projectile as it shot across the deck. It narrowly missed me but hit Billy and sent him flying over the edge." She squeezed her eyes shut. "It was an awful moment. I thought we'd lost him."

"That's why it's important to stay below deck during a storm," Phoenix said firmly, but his eyes were kind.

She knew she was being reprimanded and fair enough, as

she'd broken the rules. After two years working on rigs, she should have known better.

"I know," she said, feeling guilty. We shouldn't have gone topside. It's my fault he was knocked over. If we hadn't tried to help…" She petered off, grimacing. That was the ugly truth of it. They'd broken the rules and someone had almost died. If not for Phoenix and Boomer.

"It's not your fault," Phoenix said quickly. "That's not what I meant. You couldn't have predicted that would happen."

"Still, if we hadn't—"

"Forget it, Ellie." He reached out and wiped a wet strand of hair off her face. "I'm just glad you're okay." His touch was electric, and she froze, unsure what to do. Here he was telling her off, and rightly so, and the next moment, he's touching her, his fingers brushing against her skin. It felt… intimate.

Ellie swallowed and cleared her throat. "Thank God you guys knew what to do. You were incredible. You went after him and got him back. You saved his life." Okay, she was babbling again, trying to cover her reaction to his touch.

It was then she noticed Boomer had left the med center, presumably to go get cleaned up, and the medic had taken Billy into a treatment room. They were alone in the reception area.

His eyes, like dark blue lasers, cut through her inner turmoil.

Please don't look at me like that.

He was drawing her in, and she felt powerless to resist. The fluttering in her stomach turned into crashing waves of anticipation. Her pulse raced, and she felt the heat in his gaze —consuming her.

Oh, hell.

When this happened, she completely forgot what she

should do and gave in to what her body wanted to do. Right now, she was ashamed to admit, that was Phoenix.

She tried not to think of the way his broad shoulders hunched when he was brooding, or the way his impossibly blue eyes fixed on her face when he was listening to what she said, trying to understand why the sample results were such a problem. Even then, he'd been trying to help, trying to problem solve.

She definitely didn't want to think about how he'd sprung into action when the crane had come down, or the speed in which he and Boomer had launched that inflatable boat in the raging gale and gone after Billy, calculating the drift pattern based on her coordinates.

Phoenix cleared his throat and said, "You did good, Ellie. You kept it together and fed me the information we needed to find Billy."

"It was nothing." She'd been reading meteorological data since college.

"It wasn't nothing. I've met lots of people, better trained in these types of situations than you, who've fallen apart when the going got tough." Phoenix gave her a strange look.

Ellie realized it was pride. Her heart fluttered.

"We make a good team," he added.

We. Team.

The words echoed in her wind-swept brain, but it didn't stop a warmth spreading through her body. He thought they made a good team.

"You're shivering," Phoenix said softly.

"I'm okay." It wasn't the cold.

"Ellie…" His voice was deep and husky.

"Yes," she whispered, moving forward. Then she noticed a cut on his arm, his blood mixing with the sea water or rain covering his body. "You're injured," she stammered, distracted.

Phoenix glanced down. "That's nothing."

Now it was her turn to say, "That's not nothing. Here, let me…" She reached for some gauze in a nearby petri dish and tore open the pack. It was sterile, ready for whoever needed it next. The wound was a narrow but deep. He probably needed a stitch or two, not that he'd get that here.

"It's pretty deep. How'd it happen?"

"I'm not sure." His eyes didn't leave her face.

Hell, he was making it hard for her to concentrate, but she needed to do this, needed to help him—for once. With surprisingly steady hands, she wiped the wound clean of blood and looked around for a disinfectant. Finding it on the little trolley, alongside the petri dish, she dabbed it on the laceration.

He didn't even flinch. "I think it needs stitches."

"Nah, just tape it up," Phoenix told her. Ellie wasn't sure if he'd even looked at it yet.

"If you're sure."

"I'm sure."

Gently, she brought the edges of the wound together, holding them in place. She then applied butterfly strips across the laceration to keep the skin closed, providing a temporary hold that would encourage healing. To secure the wound further, she covered it with a sterile gauze pad and wrapped a cohesive bandage around the area, ensuring it was snug but not tight enough to impede circulation.

While she worked, she noticed several other scars on his hands and forearms, proof of the dangerous job he'd had. One was particularly bad. Round, jagged, and gleaming silver in the bright light of the med center.

Unable to help herself, she traced around it with her fingers.

"Bullet wound," Phoenix said, his voice deep and husky. "7.62 NATO round. Sniper got a piece of me in Iraq."

She glanced up. "Was it bad?"

"It was at the time." He turned his arm over before snaking it around her waist. "How'd you learn to treat wounds?"

"My mother was a nurse," she replied with a smile, remembering her mother teaching her and her sisters how to dress cuts and grazes when they were young. "We got into a lot of scrapes."

"Thanks," Phoenix murmured, when she was done. "For this."

She smiled as some of the tension eased. Doing something positive felt good. "You're welcome."

They gazed at each other for a long moment, then the door opened, and the medic emerged from the treatment room.

Phoenix released her.

"How is he?" Ellie turned away from him, her heart still pounding.

"He's got a mild concussion and is in a bit of shock, but he'll be fine."

"That's great." She'd never have been able to forgive herself if Billy had been badly injured, or worse, died. He'd been helping her, after all, when he'd gone over.

The tension drained out of her body.

What a night.

"I'd better get back up on deck," Phoenix said, his voice strangely tight.

She realized his night was just beginning.

"Phoenix... be careful up there," she blurted, unable to help herself.

His expression turned tender, and just for a heart-wrenching second, his blue eyes softened. "I will."

Then he was gone.

CHAPTER 10

This was not good.

Ever since the incident in Basra, Phoenix had steered clear of emotional attachments. He just didn't need the added complication in his life— he was dealing with enough already. But here was Ellie—smart, sassy, but at the same time damaged from a bad experience she hadn't mentioned yet—pressing all the right buttons.

As much as he was drawn to her, he couldn't let himself get close. Not after what happened to his team. That was on him. His decision, his call, his burden to bear. He didn't deserve happiness, not when his choices had cost good men their lives.

The wind howled as he patrolled the deck with Boomer, both having recovered from their rescue mission. It was close to 0600 hours now, but the storm raged on, showing no sign of letting up. The sun was a silver slit over the horizon, as if the clouds were preventing it from rising. In time, it would, and the mayhem of the night would fade into the background. But right now, the squall was still full of fury.

When he'd seen Ellie lying on the platform, clinging to the railing...

Fuck. He'd nearly lost it. She'd looked so scared, but also distressed about Billy, who'd been trying to help her secure the railing. In that moment, his only thought had been to rescue her. Only once she was safe had he and Boomer gone after the missing man.

He hadn't felt that fear since Basra. Since he'd made the call that had gotten his men killed. The guilt hit him like a punch to the gut, stealing his breath. He couldn't go through that again. Couldn't be responsible for more lives lost.

Yet that moment in the med center... Ellie tending to his wound... Her fingers light on his skin... tracing his scar.

Fuck.

Ellie deserved so much better than a man haunted by his past mistakes.

"Hey, Phoenix. Come and check this out." Boomer was calling him from the railing where Billy had fallen off.

He pushed thoughts of Ellie out of his mind.

"What's up?" He slid the mountaineering rope through his hand and joined Boomer on the windswept platform. No more chances. They'd fastened themselves to the rig, the sturdy clips connected to the pylons that jutted out from the structure. The sudden, violent gusts of wind could take even the strongest man by surprise. He knew from experience that when it came down to man versus nature, nature always won.

The rain still pelted down, stinging their faces like a million tiny needles, but it seemed less severe than earlier. Maybe the tropical storm was losing some of its power. He hoped so. It had been one fucking long night. Tension gripped his neck and shoulders, and his arm was throbbing where it had been cut. He'd probably ask the medic to give him a tetanus shot when he got off duty, just in case. What he really wanted was a hot shower and a nap, but then he knew thoughts of Ellie would intrude.

Maybe it was better he kept going until he collapsed from exhaustion. That way, he wouldn't have to think about her pale skin framed by drenched hair, her lips quivering with emotion, her eyes huge and pleading in the harsh light of the med center.

Phoenix, be careful.

Or how much he wanted to kiss her. But he couldn't let himself give in to that desire. He was damaged, a man with blood on his hands, consumed by guilt. Ellie deserved so much more. No matter how much it hurt, he had to keep his distance. For her sake.

Goddamnit.

"Look at this." Boomer pointed to the vertical join of the railing. "Several bolts are missing here. It's like they were intentionally removed."

"What?" Phoenix leaned in closer, squinting through the heavy rain. Sure enough, the bolts that should have been securing the railing were gone, leaving gaping holes in the metal. "There was nothing wrong with this railing last night, and I doubt the storm could have loosened them to the point of falling out completely."

"Agreed," Boomer said, scowling.

"You think it was sabotage?"

"Maybe. Can't be sure, but without those bolts, it was bound to come loose in the storm."

"Shit." Phoenix thought for a moment. He didn't like the direction in which his mind was going. Didn't want to think they had a saboteur—or worse—on board the rig. He turned back to Boomer. "Let's keep this to ourselves for now."

Boomer nodded. "Yeah, it may be nothing. Let's wait until the storm is over and do a thorough evaluation. We should check the other railings too."

"Good idea." They'd have to do a full risk assessment after the storm had passed, anyway. Finally, they reached the end of their shift, and two fresh security personnel took over. Both newcomers had helped during the night but had managed to get a couple of hours of sleep in the early hours after Billy had been rescued.

Heading back to their cabin, Phoenix said, "If it was sabotage, the culprit must have known the railing would come loose in the storm. He'd know he was putting lives at risk."

"That's what worries me," Boomer muttered. "Whoever did this wanted to create an incident."

"Well, it worked. We nearly lost Billy."

"But why?" Boomer asked, scratching his head.

"That is something I don't know," Phoenix replied with a weary sigh. "But I intend to find out."

CHAPTER 11

"ant another game of pool?" Suzi asked her.

Ellie shook her head. "Nah, I'm done. I think I'll go back to the lab and take another look at those samples."

While the storm blew itself out, most of the roughnecks, scientists, and analysts were stuck below deck with nothing much to do other than hang out in the recreational lounge or the mess hall. Even she couldn't work, not without fresh samples to analyze. Only the security teams were working, taking turns to make sure the drilling equipment was secure, everyone was accounted for, and no one ventured topside.

After what had happened to Billy, the private security operatives had cracked down on personnel going up, even to get fresh air. "No unauthorized access" was the phrase used, and Ellie couldn't help feeling she was somehow responsible.

Phoenix and Boomer had been pretty scarce, which was both a relief and a disappointment. After what had happened at the med center, she longed to see Phoenix again but was also scared about how she might react. She hadn't wanted a man so much in a long time, if ever, and she was desperately afraid he'd see that.

Not since Rafe.

She shuddered. What that guy had put her through. It didn't bear thinking about.

When they'd first met, she'd been very much in love. Rafe was exciting, intoxicating, and a little bit dangerous. A lot dangerous, as it turned out. But for a play-it-safe lab geek like her, he was addictive. A bad boy in every sense of the word.

Looking back, she had no idea what Rafe had seen in her. Yet, he'd gone out of his way to wine and dine her, show her a good time, and finally, seduce her.

Ellie shook her head. She should have realized he was up to no good. Too smooth, too fast-talking, too many secrets.

Even so, she hadn't wanted to claw at Rafe's clothes and strip him naked every time she saw him. She'd never had this deep-seated desire to be with him, to find out more about him, to discover what made him tick. Not like she did with Phoenix.

Ellie guessed it was her natural curiosity kicking in. Phoenix was an enigma, a puzzle, and she wanted to solve it. There was so much she didn't know about him. The only problem was, she sensed there might be something there she did not want to find. What she didn't want was to throw herself under a bus like she had before. Rafe had made her question everything. Men. Herself. Her own judgment.

It had knocked her confidence, and fast-forward two years, she was still single, still having panic attacks, and still unable to trust anyone.

Damn Rafe.

He'd really screwed her up.

Ellie looked up as the subject of her thoughts entered the room, followed closely by Boomer. Both men looked a lot more relaxed than they had earlier and were dressed casually in jeans and loose shirts, towering above everyone, easily the most handsome men in the room. Her gaze lingered on Phoenix, admiring the way his shirt hugged his toned chest and shoulders.

"Hey!" Suzi lit up like a candle and sidled over to Boomer. "I thought we weren't going to see you guys this afternoon."

"We had some stuff to do," Boomer said vaguely.

Ellie glanced at Phoenix, only to find his piercing blue eyes already focused intently on her. It made her quiver inside.

"Can I have a word?" he asked, his deep voice sending another tremor through her body.

Uh-oh. Her heart leaped into her mouth. What could he possibly want to say to her in private? Had she done something wrong? Or was this about what had happened in the med center?

"Sure." They walked a little distance away from the others. As they went, Ellie heard Suzi ask, "What's that about?"

"Not sure." Boomer gestured to the pool table. "How about a game?"

"You're on!"

"What's up?" she asked Phoenix, then gnawed on her lip, a habit she had when she was nervous.

"I need to ask you about what happened last night," he said, his voice gentle. "When Billy got swept off the platform."

"Oh, that." She let out a relieved sigh. "I thought I was in trouble."

He frowned, genuine concern in his eyes. "Why would you think that?"

"Oh, just because we were told not to go topside, not for any reason. It was out of bounds. I thought that was because of me, that it was my fault that Billy got injured."

"No, it was just dangerous, that's all. Nothing to do with

you." He reached out and squeezed her shoulder reassuringly, his touch electric even through the fabric of her shirt.

She exhaled, relieved. "Are you sure?"

"Positive. Ellie, I want you to focus on what happened last night. Can you talk me through the events leading up to Billy's accident?"

"Sure." She took a deep breath, trying to do as he asked and not focus, instead, on his piercing blue eyes inches away from hers, his day-old stubble, or how good he smelled. "We heard that almighty crash as the crane came loose and fell over. You and Boomer raced topside to check it out."

"Yeah, what made you come up too?" He tilted his head, studying her intently.

"We wanted to see if we could help. I followed Suzi up on deck. Once we got up there, we noticed the railing was loose and buffeting around in the gale. We thought it might come apart and injure someone, so I grabbed a rope, and we tried to secure it."

"That's it? Nobody told you to do it?"

"No. What's this about?" She searched his chiseled face for clues.

Phoenix lowered his voice so only she could hear, leaning in closer. She could feel the heat radiating off his hard body. "We inspected the railing this morning, and it looks like it's been tampered with. Some of the bolts holding it together were removed."

Ellie gasped, shocked by his revelation. "Deliberately removed?"

He gave a grim nod, his jaw clenched.

"I don't understand. What does that mean?" Ellie asked, her mind reeling.

"It means someone tried to sabotage the rig. They knew the railing would come loose in the storm and might injure someone," Phoenix explained.

"Do you think someone wanted to hurt Billy?" It was unthinkable, Billy was such a great guy, yet Ellie's mind was already trying to work out the puzzle, if there was one.

"Did you say Billy came to help you? That he told you to stay clear?" Phoenix questioned.

"Yes, that's right." Ellie distinctly remembered him saying that. If it wasn't for him, it would be her who'd been standing by the railing when that rogue object came hurtling toward him.

She gasped, as the revelation struck. "You don't think—?" She couldn't finish. It was too terrible for words. Too frightening.

Phoenix gave a sage nod, his expression darkening. "I think we have to consider the possibility that someone was trying to hurt you, Ellie."

Suddenly the room started to spin. She clutched her throat and gasped for breath. Phoenix frowned.

"Ellie, are you okay?" His husky voice was laced with worry.

But she couldn't respond, couldn't focus on anything except the rising panic threatening to consume her. Her shoulders heaved as she fought for air. Hoarse raspy breaths burned her lungs.

Breathe. Ellie heard her therapist's voice in her head.

In and out. In and out.

It wasn't helping. Oh, God. She was going to pass out.

Wildly, she looked for an exit. Spotting the door, she turned and ran. If she could get outside, get some air, she might be okay.

She charged for the stairs leading to the deck. She was halfway up them when strong arms lifted her off her feet.

"Ellie, stop." Phoenix grabbed her, turned her to face him. Ellie lashed out, desperate to get away, but instead of letting her go, he cradled her against his chest.

She stared up at him, still hyperventilating, her hands fisted in his shirt.

"It's okay," he said, his voice calm and soothing. "Just breathe. It will be okay. You're safe. Nothing's going to happen to you. I promise." He stroked her hair with a tenderness that made her heart ache.

She stopped fighting, focusing instead on his deep voice, his reassuring words, and slowly felt herself begin to relax. Her breathing gradually returned to normal.

"That's it," Phoenix murmured. "Nice slow breaths. I've got you."

She melted into him, allowing his strength to seep into her, chasing away the last vestiges of fear. It felt so natural, so right, to be held in his protective embrace.

Exhaustion hit her then, as it always did after one of her attacks. She slumped against him, weak and trembling, and he guided them down to sit on the metal stairs, keeping an arm securely around her. She leaned her head on his shoulder, savoring his closeness.

"You okay?" Phoenix asked, his breath warm against her hair.

"Yes. Or I will be." She felt embarrassed and vulnerable. "I'm sorry. I just... What you said, it triggered me." She tensed, waiting for him to pull away.

He must think her so silly. Here he was, this tough former SEAL, afraid of nothing, and she was having an anxiety attack because she'd nearly been hit by flying debris in a storm.

It was laughable, if it wasn't so frightening.

But Phoenix only held her tighter, his hand rubbing soothing circles on her back. "You have nothing to apologize for, Ellie. I'm here for you. I'm not going anywhere."

Tears pricked her eyes at his heartfelt words. She raised her head to look at him and whispered, "Thank you."

Phoenix brushed a strand of hair from her face, his fingers lingering on her cheek. "Don't worry. I won't let anything happen to you." His blue eyes blazed into hers.

Ellie nodded, unable to speak past the lump of emotion in her throat. How was it that she barely knew Phoenix, but when she was with him, it felt more real and right than anyone she'd been with before.

Phoenix pressed a tender kiss to her forehead then helped her to her feet. "Come on, let's get you some water and you can tell me what happened to make you react that way. Letting it out will help. I promise I'm a good listener."

Ellie sighed. After her little performance, she supposed she owed him an explanation. Nodding, she let him lead her to the cafeteria. It was practically empty, not being serving time, and they took a table by the window. The rain had stopped, and there was even some blue appearing behind the clouds.

"I had a bad experience," she began, once he'd gotten her a cup of water and she'd taken a sip. How did she tell him about Rafe? About how stupid and naive she'd been? He'd never look at her in the same way again. "It was two years ago, and sometimes I have anxiety attacks."

He sat down beside her. The chairs were close together, their legs almost touching. His closeness was reassuring—it gave her strength.

"Tell me," Phoenix said. "It'll make you feel better."

Would it? She wasn't sure about that.

Oh, hell. What did she have to lose? He'd seen her at her worst, anyway.

"There was this guy," she began.

Phoenix nodded. His face was impassive. He wasn't judging, just listening.

"I met Rafael when I got back from Saudi. He was a biker. A real bad boy." She grimaced at the phrasing, but it was true.

"I fell for him, and for a while, everything was great, but then I realized he was into some shady stuff."

Phoenix frowned. "What kind of stuff?"

"Dealing, I think. I wasn't really sure. He rode with an outlaw motorcycle club, or so he told me. I thought he was exaggerating. Turns out he wasn't." She gave a soft snort. "One day, I was at his place when the cops came around. They had a warrant for his arrest. Instead of giving himself up, he took me hostage." She swallowed, aware her voice was trembling but unable to stop it.

Phoenix took her hand across the table. "What happened?"

"He… held a knife to my throat. Threatened to kill me."

"Jesus Christ," Phoenix hissed.

"The police were pointing their guns at us, but Rafe was using me as a shield. He threatened to slice my throat. I was so scared. I thought I was going to die. I've never been that scared in my whole life."

He gave her knee a gentle squeeze. "Did they get him?"

"Yeah. He cut me on the neck to make his escape out the window, but they got him." Her fingers fluttered at her neck. "I've still got the scar."

He nodded. "I've seen it."

"Oh." She hadn't thought he'd noticed. "Anyway, the cops caught him trying to get away on his motorcycle. He's serving twelve years at San Quentin."

"What were the charges?" His face was a mask.

"Drug trafficking, GBH, attempted murder." She took a shuddering breath. "I can't believe I fell for someone like that."

"It's not your fault," Phoenix said, not for the first time.

"That's where you're wrong," she whispered. "That was my fault. I willingly dated someone I knew was wrong for me. Someone dangerous. Even my sister warned me against

72

him. I was just so bored after those years in the Middle East, I wanted a little fun, you know? I thought it would do me good." She shook her head. "I couldn't have been more wrong."

"We all make mistakes." Phoenix released her hand. She kind of liked holding it. It was comforting, like he cared.

"Some more so than others," Ellie said darkly.

He inhaled and nodded. "Yeah. Some more so than others."

CHAPTER 12

*P*hoenix stalked the deck, his hands balled into fists. Damn the bastard who'd done this to her. If the creep wasn't locked up, he'd hunt him down and beat the shit out of him. How dare he put a knife to her throat and scare the living crap out of her? What man did that?

Especially to someone as innocent as Ellie. She was a scientist. She studied elements. Wouldn't harm a fly. He knew her well enough to know that. She was dedicated, honest, and principled. She worried about her job and tried to do the right thing. Hell, she even got upset if she felt she'd broken a rule.

A weak beam of sunlight cut through the clouds, which were now dissipating. The gale had decreased to a stiff breeze, and the swells calmed to mere ripples lapping around the base of the rig.

But the transformation was lost on him. Phoenix let out an angry snort. She was a good person. Holding a knife to her throat and threatening her life was the lowest form of low. What a scumbag.

After her revelation, he'd made sure she was okay, then

came up here to get some air. Witnessing her panic attack had dug up all kinds of unwanted memories. While he'd never suffered from attacks or PTSD, he had struggled with guilt. Survivor's guilt.

Even though he'd been the cause of it.

Ellie didn't know this, but he felt her pain on a deeply personal level. He'd been there. He was no stranger to fear. He knew how it felt, eating him up inside. The difference was, for him it came with the territory. Running headfirst into danger was his job, or it had been for many years. Subsequently, he'd learned how to handle it. He'd almost become immune to it.

Obviously, he mitigated the risks. They'd been trained to do that. Volatile situations were his bread and butter. Not like Ellie. Civilians leading normal lives shouldn't have to experience the kind of fear she had. That's what law enforcement was for. That's what *they* were for.

Still, shit happened. He knew that better than most, too.

Ellie would heal, but it would take a while. Two years wasn't a long time. No wonder she'd isolated herself on an oil rig in the North Sea. It didn't get any more remote than that. She was running away, hiding from the world.

He ground his teeth. Fucking prick. He hoped Rafael was having a hellish time inside. He damn well deserved it.

Phoenix did a lap of the deck, stopping in front of the railing. He and Boomer had fixed it earlier that day, so it was no longer a hazard. Even though the wind had died down, he hadn't wanted anyone leaning against it. Or worse, falling over it. The last thing they needed was a repeat performance of last night.

Phoenix frowned, his thoughts taking a dark turn. Had Ellie been a target? Or was the whole thing just a terrible accident? Maybe he and Boomer were reading too much into this.

He thought about what Ellie had said about her sample data and how the results didn't add up. She was conscientious. He imagined her work was precise and accurate. It would match her personality. So while he knew mistakes could be made, he also knew she'd checked her samples multiple times and was still coming up empty.

That *was* weird.

He hadn't mentioned it to her because he didn't want to spook her even more, but he'd been trained to figure out anomalies, to think strategically about things, and he couldn't shake the feeling that her samples had something to do with this.

Then there was the mystery item that had shot across the platform and careened into Billy, sending him flying overboard. Along with Boomer, Phoenix had searched the deck and taken a rough inventory—everything was accounted for. So what had come loose?

He raked a hand through his hair, worried. He didn't like this. Could Ellie be at risk? Could her life be in danger?

Stiffening, he made a decision. From now on, he'd have to keep a very close eye on her—just until things settled down. He was posted out here for the duration of the project. If someone was trying to hurt her, they'd have to get through him first.

With grim determination, Phoenix turned to go back downstairs. He pitied the man who tried that.

STICKING close to Ellie was easier said than done. Now that normal rig operations had commenced and she'd received the test samples from the well, she'd locked herself in her lab and hadn't come out all afternoon.

Phoenix checked his watch. 1900 hours. He was going on duty soon and wanted to see her before he did. He told himself it was to warn her to keep an eye out for anything unusual, but deep down, he knew it was more than that. His feelings for her were growing, despite his efforts to keep them at bay. He wanted to protect her, to keep her safe from harm, but he couldn't let her know how much he cared.

He wanted to check if she was okay, that she hadn't had any more panic attacks, that she'd recovered from the earlier incident.

When had he started caring so much?

It was now or never. He stopped pacing outside her lab and knocked on the door.

"Come in."

He twisted the handle and went inside.

She swiveled around on her chair. "Hey, Phoenix."

The moment he walked into the room, he could tell something was bothering her. "Hey, I just wanted to see how you were."

"I'm okay, thanks." She managed a weak smile. "I got the test samples today, and I've been going through them. To be honest, I've gone through them several times."

"And?" he prompted, guessing it wasn't good news.

She sighed, her slender shoulders sagging. "It's the same as the others. No hydrocarbons. I can't find any trace of viable oil deposits in this area. It just doesn't make sense."

He frowned. "What exactly does this mean?"

"It means there's no oil here. There never was. I don't care what the geological surveys say. This is not a commercially viable reserve."

He put his hands on his hips and stared at her, deep in thought. Eventually, he asked, "Is that usual?"

"What do you mean?"

"I mean, is it usual to not find reserves despite what the geological surveys say?"

"Not really. I mean, some sites have more potential than

others, but usually, the samples back up what the geological data says."

He exhaled, his heart aching at the sight of her distress. All he wanted to do was pull her into his arms and tell her everything would be okay, that he would protect her no matter what. But he couldn't. He had to keep his distance, to remain professional.

"What are you thinking, Phoenix?"

"I don't know. It might be nothing, but do you think there's something wrong with this situation?"

She sat quietly, studying him. "You mean, could there be something shady going on?"

"Yeah, like with the survey reports or the samples?"

"I don't know. I suppose there could be. I mean, the surveys are extensive and conducted by a reputable company, but there's a possibility they're incorrect." She thought for a moment. "There is another way to check, but it would involve getting surveys from another organization and comparing the two."

"Can you do that?" he asked.

"I can, but there'll be questions asked. If you mean, can I do it under the radar? I don't know. I could try."

"In light of everything that's happened, I think it's a good idea if you don't tell anyone about this yet. If the survey reports are the same, then no harm done, but if they're not... well, then we have to bring that to someone's attention."

Ellie paled. "I can't believe anyone would deliberately—"

"They may not have," he said quickly. "You said yourself, it's just a way of double-checking the data."

She gave a small nod. "Okay, but I'll have to tell Suzi. She's a geologist, and she'll know who we can contact for a fresh set of reports."

"Okay, but no one else," he warned her, hoping he was

wrong. It was just that this damn suspicion wouldn't go away.

"It's late now, so it'll have to be tomorrow." Ellie rose and stretching her neck.

He saw the tiny scar the knife blade had made as it caught the light and felt a renewed flush of anger. No one would hurt her again. At least, not on his watch. He would do everything in his power to keep her safe, even if it meant hiding his feelings. She could never know how much he cared, how much he wanted to be more than just her protector.

But unfortunately, that's all he could ever be.

CHAPTER 13

*E*llie was sitting quietly in her room reading a book when Suzi waltzed in, flushed and excited. Best guess—her roommate had spent the whole afternoon with Boomer.

"I really like him," Suzi confessed, eyes bright. "You know, he told me Phoenix hasn't been with anyone since he left the SEALs."

"Really?" She tried to act disinterested, but her ears pricked up.

"Yeah, Boomer said Phoenix took a real knock after what happened in Basra, and he hasn't been the same since."

"Basra?" Ellie frowned. "What happened in Basra?"

"I don't know," Suzi admitted. "Boomer wouldn't say, but I think something really bad went down. It must have been for Phoenix to check out of the Navy."

Her curiosity was piqued. Phoenix had never mentioned Iraq or given a reason why he'd left the Navy. When she'd asked, he simply said it was time. A very vague answer, by all accounts.

"Well, I'm sure he had his reasons," she said, trying to sound nonchalant.

Suzi gave her a sly smile. "How are you two getting on?"

"Fine. To be honest, I've been so busy with the test samples, I haven't seen him much today." Except for when he'd come to her lab and warned her that someone might be trying to harm her and it might have something to do with the oil reserves or lack thereof.

"I've just seen him," Suzi told her. "He and Boomer have gone on their shift. At least the storm has passed. It's much warmer topside now."

"Yeah, that's a relief." The last two days had been fraught with fear, anxiety, and frustration. She was glad things were getting back to normal.

Earlier that evening, after Phoenix had left her lab, she had contacted her friend, Ray, at Stanford. At first, he'd been reluctant to help, but when he'd heard why she needed the information, he'd said he'd look into it. There might be a way of accessing the satellite imaging data through the college's account.

She'd given him the relevant coordinates and asked him to call her back on her cell when he had something. Now it was just a waiting game.

Exhausted from the last few days, she fell asleep early, which is why she was wide awake at a quarter to five the next morning. Her first thought was to check her phone, but there were no messages from Ray.

Her second thought was to venture up on deck and stretch out the tension of the last few days. The added bonus was she'd get to see Phoenix. She could tell him she'd contacted Ray, and he was going to try to help her.

Careful not to wake Suzi, Ellie dressed in her yoga gear, grabbed her mat , hung her ID badge around her neck, and went up to the deck.

The sea was calm, the sky a deep indigo but lightening in the east, and there was not a cloud in sight. It promised to be a beautiful day. Ellie looked around but couldn't spot Phoenix or Boomer, so she laid her mat on the helipad, stretched, then broke into her routine.

She was halfway through a downward-facing dog when Phoenix appeared behind her. She straightened up, but not before she caught him checking out her ass. Hard not to, really, in that position.

"Morning." Somehow, he managed to keep his expression neutral, but Ellie could see a naughty sparkle in his gaze.

"Morning," she replied, willing her cheeks not to turn pink. At least the sun had only begun to rise, so there was still a misty predawn haze in the air. There were more important matters to discuss than her butt. "I managed to contact my friend."

"Oh, yeah?" He stood at the end of her mat, large hands holding his weapon, broad shoulders relaxed but straining against the dark long-sleeved shirt he wore under his tactical vest. Even in the dim light, the defined muscles of his arms, honed from years of intense training and combat were visible. "What did he say?"

"He's going to try to use the college link to access the feed."

"Good. Will that give you the information you need?"

"It will, yes. I can compare it with the survey report and make sure everything's above board."

"You didn't tell anyone what you were doing?"

"No, I called when Suzi was out, so nobody knows."

"Excellent. Good job. Keep me posted."

"I will."

He gestured to the yoga mat. "I'll let you get back to your routine."

Ellie hesitated. He hadn't moved away. Did that mean he

was going to watch? His intense blue gaze roamed over her for a moment, and she felt the familiar swirling in her stomach.

As if catching himself, he muttered, "Sorry, I'm going now," and continued his patrol around the deck, disappearing behind a mesh of pylons.

Exhaling, she tried to focus her attention on the moves and not the lingering image of him checking her out. His appraisal had left her feeling self-conscious and exposed, but at the same time hot and bothered. Part of her wanted to cross her arms in front of her body and hide, while another, wilder part wanted to rip off her clothes and press his big, strong hands against her skin.

Her pulse raced again. Hardly the calm workout she'd envisioned.

Still, Ellie gritted her teeth and went through the motions, determined not to give in to the raw, unbridled desire that consumed her whenever Phoenix was nearby.

She had to exercise some control over her emotions. She was a scientist, for Pete's sake. Logic ruled her head, *not* passion. She couldn't remember ever feeling this way about a guy before. Not even Jeremy Johnson, her first crush in high school.

That had been a hurried kiss behind the grandstands, followed by a disappointing prom night where they'd only gotten to first base. She'd had a couple of boyfriends in college, nobody memorable. Then came three dry years in Saudi, followed by Rafael. He'd been her first real boyfriend. And her last.

Ellie bit her lip. Now all she did was run away from men. From danger. From freaking everything. It was dismal. She was too scared to live in case something bad might happen.

A harsh laugh escaped her.

Phoenix *was* danger. He'd been a Navy SEAL, trained to

be a lethal weapon, where his job was running headfirst into the most perilous situations imaginable. Now he was a private security contractor—not much better. Look what had happened the night Billy had fallen into the ocean. It was Phoenix and Boomer who'd gone after him without hesitation, risking their own lives in the process.

Holy hell. She needed her head read.

What was she doing lusting after a man like *him*? A man who embodied the very things that terrified her.

Surely he would only add more danger to her life. More risk. More fear.

Ellie exhaled, returning to the start position, her hands pressed together in front of her, but she felt anything but calm.

To still her beating heart, she remembered how Phoenix had held her during her panic attack. His strong arms enveloping her, making her feel safe and protected. How he'd soothed her with his hands, surprisingly gentle despite the calluses earned from years of handling weapons and engaging in brutal hand-to-hand combat. How he'd whispered to her, his deep voice soft and reassuring, telling her everything was going to be all right.

And it had worked.

She'd believed him.

For some strange reason, this hardened warrior, this man who was never far from his semi-automatic rifle and had faced death countless times, had been able to stop her anxiety in its tracks with a simple touch and a few comforting words.

It defied logic. The irony was almost laughable.

CHAPTER 14

*G*oddammit.

Wasn't it enough that she was the smartest woman he knew? Did she have to be the sexiest too? Bending over like that in her skin-tight leggings, her perfectly formed butt sticking up into the air...

Fuck.

He'd had a hard time keeping it together. Hell, an entire insurgency could have boarded the rig and he wouldn't have noticed. That's how distracting she was.

Phoenix shifted his weight, trying to focus on his patrol duties. But his mind kept drifting back to Ellie. Quite the contradiction too. On the one hand she was focused and dedicated, working tirelessly to prove herself in this job. On the other, she was a free spirit, dancing around the helipad, her hair blowing loosely in the breeze.

She protected herself by being reserved, quiet, and burying herself in her work, but when he'd surprised her that first morning, she'd turned into a hellcat, spitting fire at him and glaring through terrified tiger's eyes.

She was both fire and ice, confident and fearful. Which

meant he wanted to protect her and rip her clothes off in the same goddamned breath.

He knew now that her crazed effort to fight back that first morning was because of her ex, the scumbag who had held her hostage. After yesterday's panic attack, he'd realized the depth of her fear, but he knew that hiding away from it didn't help.

Wasn't he a good one to talk? He was hiding too. Not from fear, but from facing up to what he'd done. Seemed they each had a cross to bear.

Still, she'd obviously taken self-defense classes because she'd fought back admirably. In most cases, she'd have gotten away. He wasn't most cases.

Then there was the imagined threat. He still didn't know if he was being paranoid, or if she really had been a target up there on the deck near the railing.

There was no doubt the bolts had been removed. He and Boomer had poured over the security camera footage on the deck, but annoyingly it didn't pick up that section. Could the saboteur have known? Was that why that area had been chosen? In which case, whomever was responsible must have been familiar with the angle of the security cameras. Only someone with access would be. Boomer was going to talk to the other guys and put together a list.

At least the helipad was covered. He'd made sure of that. While Ellie went through her morning routines, the beady eye attached to the top of the crane was recording her every move. And the moves of anyone else who might be out there. The feed wasn't manned at all times, but it could be played back if necessary. He hoped it would never come to that.

Phoenix watched her from the shadows. In his dark attire, with wide steel structures between him and the helipad, he was practically invisible. Ellie, however, was standing on the highest point of the rig, bathed in gentle sunbeams.

He watched as her hair caught the light, turning it a deep golden brown. Her skin seemed to shimmer in the incandescent glow as she turned and stared out to sea. What was she thinking?

About him?

His ego hoped she was, but a more sensible side prayed she wasn't. He was not the type of man she needed, especially not after her last experience. She needed a nice calm scientist or tech geek to discuss clever things with. Non-dangerous arms to hold her as she fell asleep at night. Someone placid and boring. Someone safe.

The thought made him physically ill.

At some point over the last few days, he'd begun to think of her as his. And that was a very, very bad idea. He couldn't allow himself to get attached, not with his track record, not with the demons of his past still haunting him. She deserved better than a broken man like him.

But God, he wanted her. Wanted to taste her lips, feel her soft skin underneath his rough hands. He imagined pulling her close, his hands roaming her curves as she melted into his embrace.

No. He shook his head, trying to dispel the fantasy. He had to focus on protecting her, on keeping her safe from whoever was targeting her out here—if anyone was targeting her. That was his job, his mission. He couldn't let his attraction get in the way.

Phoenix tore his gaze from Ellie and resumed his patrol. He had a job to do, and his feelings couldn't enter into it. She was his to protect, even if she could never truly be his.

"What are you looking so gloomy about?" Boomer said, surprising him. He'd been so distracted he hadn't heard his colleague approach. That was a first.

"Nothing. Just mulling over the loose railing."

"That's what I wanted to tell you," Boomer said. "Blake in

the security room called me over the radio. The only people who have access to the surveillance cameras are us four operatives, Billy, the Ops Manager, and Henderson, the boss. Nobody else is allowed in."

"So, it had to be one of those people?" Phoenix said, frowning. "I can't see Billy sabotaging the railing and then falling over it, can you?"

Boomer shook his head. "Not unless he wanted to play the hero to impress Ellie."

Hmm… that could be. "Pretty extreme lengths to go to impress a girl. I can think of easier ways."

"Yeah." Boomer shrugged it off.

"What about Henderson?" Phoenix asked. "Could he have done it?"

"I mean, he could have, but why would he want to sabotage his own project? He's got a lot riding on this. Like his career."

Phoenix sighed. "Yeah, it's not likely to be him either."

"And it's not any of us. We're being paid to ensure those kinds of things don't happen."

"Which leaves us with what?" Phoenix squinted across the deck. The risen sun had turned the sea into a mirror. He couldn't see Ellie anymore. She must have gone back down to get ready for her day.

"Maybe it was an accident," Boomer suggested. "The storm could have worked the bolts loose."

"Yeah, maybe."

But neither of them believed it.

CHAPTER 15

*E*llie had just entered the lab when her phone rang. It was Ray!

After locking the door, she settled down on her ergonomic swivel chair and took the call. "Ray, thanks for getting back to me."

"I've got that data you wanted, Ellie. How'd you want to do this?"

"Can you share your screen with me?"

"Yeah, let's talk via Zoom. I'll send you a link."

She logged on to her high-performance computer just as Ray sent the invitation. After clicking on the link, the familiar screen popped up and she was facing her old college buddy. Ray, unlike her, had never left university. A true academic, he'd opted to study further and had applied to Stanford. He was now a professor of geological sciences.

"Sharing in progress," he said.

A satellite image filled her expansive, high-resolution monitor. Swirls of red, orange, and yellow were surrounded by cool greens and blues like an abstract Van Gogh painting.

She took a long, hard look. A nagging thought plagued her, but she couldn't figure out what it was.

"It's so strange," she said, finally. "From this, I wouldn't have said there were oil reserves beneath us at all, yet the reports we got say there are." Then it clicked. The rock structures on the reports looked different from what she was seeing on the screen.

"This is live, isn't it?" she asked, a little breathless.

Ray grunted. "Yeah, this is a satellite image of the seabed and surrounding rock formations based on those coordinates you gave me. I'm feeding it directly from the satellite."

"Would you mind if I printed off a copy of this?" she asked. "I can take a screenshot."

"Go for it. If you need it for your work—"

"Thanks." She hit print and the high-end color printer beside her whirred to life. Shortly after, a crisp, standard-size image emerged.

Ellie stared at the images on the screen for a bit longer.

"What are you thinking?" asked Ray, breaking the silence.

"I'm not sure." Ellie frowned, then shook her head. "I think I have to compare this to what I have here."

"Okay, no problem. Let me know if you need anything else."

"Thanks, Ray. I appreciate it."

"Anytime, Ellie. You take care now."

"You too." He ended the call.

She unlocked the lab door then darted into the corridor. The drills were silent now, as she had her test samples. In a day or two, they'd move on to the fifth test site and commence drilling there.

Except, what she'd just learned might change everything.

Ellie glanced at the image in her hand then hurried to the control center. Inside, she approached a technician monitoring numerous screens displaying real-time data and asked if he'd seen Suzi. He shook his head.

She tried the gym, the mess hall, and their room, but Suzi wasn't in any of them. There was only one other place she could be, and that was with Henderson.

Ellie had worked up a sweat by the time she got to their boss's office. In utter contrast to her sleek, modern lab and the busy control center, he was allocated a small cubicle with a dirty porthole for a window, which looked past layers of scaffolding to the ocean beyond. The door was ajar, and she could hear her boss's voice emanating from inside.

"It has to be tomorrow," he was saying.

Ellie knocked. He fell silent.

She pushed open the door and both Suzi and Henderson spun around to look at her. "Sorry to interrupt, but I really need to see those reports again, Suzi."

"Oh. Hi, Ellie. Of course. I'll just go and get them." She turned back to Henderson. "Okay, I'll let the Operations Manager know we've got the new coordinates."

"What's the rush?" Suzi asked as they marched back along the corridor to her office.

"Something about the rock formations on the satellite images," Ellie panted, still trying to catch her breath. "They look different from those on your reports."

"What satellite images?" Suzi asked, frowning.

Shit, she'd forgotten she hadn't told her about Ray.

"The ones I asked a friend to source for us. He's a professor at Stanford, and he managed to tap into a live satellite feed for me."

"He did?" Suzi frowned. She looked surprised.

"Yeah. I had to know if we were working with the right survey data, Suzi. You understand, don't you?" Hopefully, her new friend wouldn't be too upset that she'd gone behind her back.

"Yes, of course. Sorry, I was just surprised, that's all. I didn't realize you went to Stanford."

Ellie laughed. "He did, not me. Anyway, I thought we'd better check since I'm getting so many anomalies. And I swear the satellite images are showing something different."

Suzi shook her head. "I don't understand."

"Me neither. Let's get the reports so we can compare."

"Okay."

They grabbed the folder then ran back to the lab.

"Look." Ellie placed the printout from the satellite image next to the identical one in Suzi's report.

Suzi studied them both. As a geologist, she was best placed to recognize the differences in the rock strata beneath the seabed. "You're right," she whispered, her voice strained. "The underwater rock structure and the sea bottom morphology are different."

Ellie stared at her, triumphant. "I knew there was something wrong."

"What does it mean?" Suzi asked.

"It means this is a different location from the one in the survey," said Ellie breathlessly. "It means we've been drilling in the wrong place."

"How can it be?" Suzi whispered, once the initial shock had worn off.

"I don't know," Ellie rubbed her forehead. The beginning of a headache pricked behind her eyes, "but I'm going to have to take this to Henderson."

"Oh, my God. This is huge," Suzi's face was pale. "It means we were sent the wrong data. Our entire project was based on that. It's going to involve a full-scale investigation. The project will be halted. We'll both lose our jobs."

"I know." The implications weren't lost on her. If the geographical data provided by the survey company was incorrect, it could have severe consequences for the entire oil exploration project. The company had invested millions of dollars based on this data, and if it turned out to be faulty, it could lead to significant financial losses and legal repercussions.

Moreover, an investigation into the survey company would likely uncover the reasons behind the incorrect data. Was it a simple mistake, or was there something more sinister at play like Phoenix had suggested? The possibility of intentional manipulation or corruption within the survey company was a serious concern that she couldn't ignore.

Maybe she should tell someone? Except whom? She didn't know how high this went. Henderson might be involved, in which case she was putting herself at risk by going to him. Suzi didn't want to be the whistleblower, especially since she depended on this job for her living.

They all did.

Ellie spent the rest of the day writing up her report. She knew once the investigation was launched, she'd have to back up her claim. That meant having irrefutable evidence, including double-checking her own data analysis, and referencing Ray's Stanford satellite images.

As she worked on her report, she couldn't help but think about the potential fallout from this discovery. The oil exploration project was a large undertaking, involving numerous stakeholders, from investors to local authorities. If the project was derailed due to the incorrect geographical data, it could have far-reaching effects on everyone involved.

Plus, the investigation into the survey company could open up a Pandora's box of corporate malfeasance and corruption. If it was revealed that the company had deliberately provided false data, it would not only destroy their reputation but could also lead to criminal charges and a loss of trust in the entire industry.

She sighed, the weight of the responsibility heavy on her

shoulders. Her report would be the catalyst for this investigation. She had to ensure her evidence was airtight and her
analysis was beyond reproach. The future of the project,
including her own career, depended on it.

CHAPTER 16

*A*s he had one night earlier, Phoenix stopped by Ellie's lab before he got ready to go on duty. As expected, she sat at her desk, but instead of working, she stared dolefully into space.

"That bad?" he asked, entering the lab.

She blew a stray hair out of her face. "You have no idea."

Phoenix took a seat opposite her and leaned back, stretching out his legs. "You got the new satellite images?"

With a nod, she told him what they'd discovered and the implications. It was bad. Really bad.

A dark suspicion grew in his gut. "This could be why you were targeted," he said quietly. "Someone was afraid of what you'd discover."

Her eyes widened, and he saw her catch her breath. "You really think so?" Her voice was a whisper.

"There is no doubt the railing was deliberately sabotaged. The crash brought everyone up on deck, and if it wasn't for Billy coming to help you, you'd have been hit by the mystery object and washed out to sea."

She was weaker than Billy, probably not as strong a

swimmer. She may not have made it before he'd gotten to her. Phoenix went cold at the thought. The more he considered it, the more he knew he was right. Someone was out to kill Ellie—and this was the reason why. "Think of what's at stake here. Not only the project but people's careers, the company's reputation, and millions of dollars in investment."

She swallowed, and he could see her chest heaving as she tried to keep her breathing under control. Ellie stared at him, eyes wide, filled with a silent plea for help, to him to make it right.

If only he could.

"What should I do, Phoenix? I can't keep quiet about this."

"I agree." He was thinking hard. "Do you have enough data to prove the survey reports were false?"

"I think so, although it help if I had another way to verify the reports are false. Two sources are better than one."

"Is there any other way you can check them?" he asked.

"Well, there is another exploratory rig operating in the eastern Gulf. I picked it up on the radar scanner yesterday. I guess I could pay them a visit and check our survey maps against theirs."

He frowned. "Can't you hop on a Zoom call?"

"I could, but they're our direct competitors. I'm not sure they'd be open to sharing information unless I was actually there."

She was right. With permits for the eastern Gulf rarer than gold dust and competition rife, it was unlikely they'd share information unless they thought it was beneficial to them. Still, he didn't like the thought of her going alone. "Will they let you on the rig?"

"I won't say who I am until I'm onboard."

He hesitated. "I'll come with you. You can't take the inflatable out alone."

"Suzi offered to come with me," she said weakly, "but it would be great having you with us."

"Oh, crap." He dropped his head into his hands.

"What?"

"I can't. I've been tasked with fixing the blowout preventer on the rig tomorrow morning. It became unstable during the storm, and Billy wants us to take a look at it."

"No worries," she said gamely, but he could see by her eyes that she was upset. No, not upset. Scared. And that tore him apart. Fuck it. If only he could get her off this rig right now and take her somewhere safe. Just the two of them.

Except that wasn't an option.

"I'll try to get out of it." He clenched his jaw. Ellie was more important. She needed him, and he wanted to be there for her. Hell, he'd never be able to live with himself if something happened to her.

"Only if you're sure."

"I'm sure."

"Absolutely not," Henderson told him. "I can't spare you. Blake and Peterson are on security duty, and I need you and Boomer on the blowout preventer. It can't wait. We're being towed to the new test site tomorrow, and it has to be operational before then."

"I don't feel comfortable letting Ellie go by herself," Phoenix tried, his gut twisting. He wasn't used to disobeying orders from a superior, but this was different. This was Ellie.

His woman.

He swallowed hard and glared at Henderson, but his boss didn't budge. "Ellie and Suzi are quite capable of doing it by themselves Ellie is a smart girl, and this isn't her first rodeo. Suzi is incredibly competent too. Don't worry about them. Report to Billy, and he'll show you where the damage is."

"Yes, sir."

Fuck.

There was no way around it. Unless he wanted to directly disobey Henderson, which might mean the end of his job, he had no choice but to fall in line.

Leaving the office, he headed topside to tell Ellie the bad news.

But he was too late.

The inflatable was already heading out into the big blue, and he could see the slim figure of Ellie at the motor. His heart leaped into his throat. Where the hell was Suzi? Why was Ellie alone?

He charged down to the launch pad and grabbed one of the roughnecks by the arm. "Why is she going out alone?"

"I don't know, man." He shrugged his arm free. "I just do as I'm told."

"Sorry." Phoenix stared after the departing figure of Ellie. "I thought she had someone going with her, that's all."

"Feisty one, isn't she?" the roughneck said, approvingly. "I wouldn't have taken that little inflatable out by myself, but then I can't swim very well."

Phoenix ground his jaw.

Where the hell was Suzi?

A throbbing noise in the sky drew his attention, and he saw the transfer chopper coming in to land. A small group of passengers accumulated on deck. He'd forgotten it was Friday, the day that many of the staff and shift workers left to go back to the mainland for the weekend. They'd be back on Monday. Activity on the rig quieted down over the weekend. From what Henderson had said, they were using this quiet period to tow the rig into its new position. New incorrect position—based on false survey data.

But Henderson didn't know that. Not yet.

Once Ellie's report landed on his desk, he'd have a heart

attack. Unless he was somehow involved. Was that possible? Could Henderson be behind the sabotage? Had he plotted to kill Ellie to silence her? Phoenix scowled at the chopper as he considered this. The man's job was at stake, and he was probably being paid a lot to oversee this project. If it fell through and there was an investigation, he'd be the obvious scapegoat.

A hard ball of fear tightened in his chest as he watched the chopper land. To his surprise, Suzi was one of the people waiting to board.

"Hey, Suzi!" he yelled, running over to her. She stood clutching her backpack, a drawn expression on her face. "Wait up!"

She turned, hearing his voice. "Phoenix, what's up?"

"Where are you going?"

Her shoulders slumped. "Back to the mainland. I got an emergency call this morning. My father had a bad fall and is in the hospital. I've got to go."

"Oh, sorry to hear that. I thought you were joining Ellie?"

"I wanted to, but she insisted she was okay. Actually, she said you were going with her."

Shit.

"I can't. I've got to fix something before the rig is towed to the new location."

She gave a distracted nod. People were climbing on board the chopper, its rotors having come to a stop. "Sorry, Phoenix. I've got to go. Say goodbye to Boomer for me."

"Sure." He stood back as she got onto the chopper with everybody else. It was a full flight, and the second one of the day. The place would be practically deserted now.

Still, that was probably a good thing. The fewer people on board, the less chance of something happening to Ellie. He could keep a close eye on Henderson, and he'd be working with Billy, not that he suspected the Ops Manager. There weren't many others who could be responsible for what had happened.

Yet, the gut-wrenching feeling he had when he turned to look at the inflatable disappearing into the shimmering distance wouldn't go away. Ellie was alone out there, vulnerable and exposed to the elements and whoever was targeting her.

Goddammit. He couldn't handle the thought of her being in danger and having no one to protect her. Unable to help himself, he let out a growl venting his helplessness and frustration.

Worse, she'd think he'd let her down. That he hadn't shown up.

Why had she gone so early? Why hadn't she told him?

Damn her stubborn independence. She probably hadn't wanted to bother him with the change in plans.

He clenched his fists, his mind racing. SEAL training had taught him to consider all scenarios, especially the worst-case ones. Plan for the worst, hope for the best, that had been his motto.

What if the saboteur had followed her out there? What if they had tampered with the inflatable, causing it to malfunction or capsize in the treacherous waters? Ellie was a strong and capable woman, but even she had her limits. The open sea could be unforgiving, and if something happened to her, he might never know until it was too late.

Phoenix took a deep breath. He had to calm the fuck down. He had to trust in Ellie's abilities and pray that she would return safely. In the meantime, he had a job to do.

And a mystery to solve.

CHAPTER 17

*E*llie checked her GPS and set a course to the Discoverer. It was roughly fifteen miles away, and by her estimation, would take thirty minutes to get there. She had enough gas for three times that distance, so there and back should be no problem whatsoever.

The sea was calm and glassy, and with the sun shining down on her back, she almost felt at peace.

Almost.

If it wasn't for the falsified survey data, the sensitive nature of her task ahead, or the fact that someone was probably trying to kill her, things would be just peachy.

She could really have used some company today. What a shame Suzi had to go back to the mainland, although it was terrible news about her father, of course. Ellie had no idea what had happened to Phoenix. Yesterday, he'd seemed pretty adamant that he was coming with her, but maybe he couldn't get out of that repair job he'd been talking about. Henderson, as she had learned, could be a hard taskmaster.

She wiped a bead of sweat from her face and stared

ahead, waiting for the hulking shape of the Discoverer to appear out of the shimmering haze. As long as she stuck to the coordinates, and her discussion with the geologist on board went according to plan, she should be back before lunchtime.

While she was anxious to compare both the survey reports and Ray's live data with the Discoverer's, she couldn't help feeling a sense of irritation that she was in this position. How typical. Her first leadership role and this happens.

What were the odds? Considering the train wreck that her life had been up until this point, she shouldn't have been surprised. Then a thought struck her.

Had she been a patsy? If this was some giant fraudulent scheme, had they purposely hired someone like her to oversee it, hoping her inexperience would mean she didn't question the survey reports too deeply?

Suddenly, she felt sick. Here she was, desperate for a job, fresh out of a two-year stint in the North Sea where she'd been part of a team of analysts, catapulted to chief engineer on the Explorer, an exploratory rig in the Gulf of Mexico. There's no way she should have gotten this job. In fact, she'd been surprised when they'd given it to her.

Her heart sank as the realization crashed over her like a tidal wave. They'd only hired her to fail.

And when she hadn't, when she'd started asking questions about the anomalies in the data, they'd tried to stage an "accident" to get rid of her.

Ellie's heart pounded in her chest, and she found it hard to breathe. Panic rose, choking her, as her mind raced with a thousand frantic thoughts. The betrayal, the danger, the uncertainty—it all swirled together in a dizzying maelstrom that threatened to overwhelm her.

Her hands shook as she gripped the tiller, her knuckles

turning white with the force of her grip. Her pulse raced, blood roaring in her ears as her breath came in short, sharp gasps. It was all she could do to keep the inflatable on course, her vision blurring as tears of frustration and fear pricked at the corners of her eyes.

Not now.

She couldn't lose it out here in the middle of nowhere.

Ellie forced herself to take a deep breath, closing her eyes for a moment as she tried to calm the chaos in her mind. She pictured Phoenix, his strong, steady presence a lifeline in the storm of her emotions.

She could almost feel his arms around her, his voice a soothing murmur in her ear.

It's okay. I've got you.

In her mind's eye, she saw his face. Got lost in those piercing blue eyes that always seemed to see right through her, to the heart of who she was. She remembered the way he'd held her during that last panic attack, his touch gentle but firm, anchoring her to reality.

She focused on the memory of his hands, rough and calloused but always so careful when he touched her. She imagined the warmth of his skin against hers, the way his fingers would trace the lines of her face, brushing away the tears that threatened to fall.

Slowly, gradually, her heartbeat began to slow. Her breathing evened out as the panic receded. The shaking in her hands subsided, and the world around her came back into focus.

She took another deep breath, letting it out slowly as she opened her eyes. She still felt shaky, but the worst of the attack had passed. She was back in control.

And it was all thanks to Phoenix. Even though he wasn't here with her physically, the thought of him had been enough to pull her back from the brink. Somehow, his strength, his steadiness, had become a part of her, something she could rely on when everything else seemed to be falling apart.

Up ahead, the gray form of the Discoverer loomed into view. She was nearly there. She squared her shoulders and pushed the inflatable as fast as she dared. Given what she now suspected, it was more important than ever that she get onboard and verify the data.

But once she'd verified it, who did she report it to? Henderson could well be involved. He was the one who'd hired her. A flush of anger made her grimace. How dare he think she was a pushover? Well, she was going to show him. As soon as she got back, she'd speak to Phoenix and together they could contact head office, or maybe they could contact someone in his organization and ask them what to do. Surely, they'd know how to handle something of this magnitude. The most important thing now was not to let Henderson know she was on to him.

Pulling up alongside the Discoverer, she gestured to one of the roughnecks manning the launch station. He beckoned for her to moor, and she threw him the rope to fasten to the makeshift dock.

The Discoverer was larger than the Explorer, but not by much. In fact, the two rigs were very similar in design, with their towering derricks rising high above the main deck, and the sprawling matrix of pipes, valves, and machinery that made up the drill floor. Like the Explorer, the Discoverer was equipped with state-of-the-art technology for deep-sea drilling and exploration, including advanced seismic imaging systems and remotely operated vehicles for underwater surveying.

She guessed they'd also be on skeleton crew due to the weekend, which meant fewer prying eyes as she made her way to the geologist's office. But as she climbed onto the deck, a sense of unease settled in the pit of her stomach.

The stakes had just gotten a whole lot higher. And if her suspicions were correct, she wasn't just fighting for her job anymore.

She was fighting for her life.

CHAPTER 18

*P*hoenix's hands gripped the ladder rungs of the rig's underbelly, his palms slick with sweat. It was a scorching hot day, but at least he was done. The blowout protector was fixed, and he could relax for a while before going on shift later tonight.

After Ellie had left on the inflatable that morning, he'd found Boomer and told him his suspicions. Boomer agreed it was possible Ellie's interest in the geographical anomalies had put her in the firing line. Like Phoenix, he was worried about her safety. They'd decided that when she got back, they'd escalate the issue, have the project shut down, and get Ellie to safety.

It couldn't happen soon enough for his liking.

As he climbed, he instinctively knew how much time had passed since she'd left. Twisting his neck, he peered out to sea, hoping to spy the inflatable coming in. So far, nothing. Not even a speck in the distance.

His gut tightened. He hoped to hell she was okay.

It would take half an hour to get there, another half an hour back, and however long it took to check the survey data with their on-board geologist. Of course, she'd have to sweet talk her way on then ask for their help—but he couldn't imagine they'd refuse a woman alone on an inflatable boat.

She should be back by now. He'd give her another half an hour and then he'd take the second inflatable and go and look for her. The only reassurance he had was that no one had left the rig that he knew of. Henderson hadn't made an appearance since this morning and was probably still holed up in his stuffy office. Unlike the shift staff, the boss rarely went back to the mainland on weekends.

Giving up on seeing Ellie return, he continued his climb to the top of the platform. Halfway up, a strip of duct tape wrapped around one of the support beams caught his eye. What the hell was that? It looked makeshift, like someone had tried to tape up a section of the beam. Leaning off the ladder, he took a closer look. He could see around the back of the beam now, where a rectangular object had been fixed to the structure.

His breath hitched, and an icy chill went down his back.

It couldn't be…

But as he moved closer, the tangle of wires, container, and duct tape confirmed his worst fear. It was an improvised explosive device. He'd seen enough of them during his time in the Middle East to recognize it.

Heart pounding, he swung off the ladder and on to the scaffolding to take a closer look. Scrambling across the support beams, he maneuvered his way underneath the rig, his eyes never leaving the device.

Sweat beaded on his forehead as he studied the bomb, searching for the trigger. Was there a timer? Or was it a remote activation? The plastic holder concealed the explosive material, making it impossible to determine the type or quantity. His mouth went dry at the implications. This wasn't just sabotage. It was complete destruction. Whoever was defrauding the company was getting desperate. Their ploy to get rid of Ellie hadn't worked, and now she'd verified the survey reports and was preparing to go public with what she knew, they were out of options.

They'd taken drastic steps to hide the evidence. A blast would destroy her samples, her data, everything—and send the rig to the bottom of the Gulf.

Phoenix's mind raced, his SEAL training kicking in. Basic IED composition, yes, but disarming the device was too risky. He didn't have the expertise. Booby-traps designed to prevent tampering were a real threat. There was only one man onboard who could disarm this bomb, and that was Boomer.

He scrambled back onto the deck, adrenaline surging through his veins. Spotting Billy tidying up, he called out, his voice steady despite the urgency. "Where's Boomer?"

Billy shrugged. "I thought he was with you."

"No, he came up twenty minutes ago."

Billy looked around. "There he is. Hey, Boomer! You're needed over here."

Thank fuck. He wasn't far.

Boomer ran over. "What's up?"

Phoenix lowered his voice. "There's a fucking IED attached to the bottom of the platform."

The explosive expert's eyes widened. "You're kidding?"

Phoenix shook his head. "We've got to get everybody off this rig, pronto."

Boomer's jaw clenched, and he nodded. "Let me take a look."

Phoenix went to talk to Billy while Boomer hurried to the ladder.

The Ops Manager's eyes grew wide as the implications dawned on him. "Okay, I'll sound the alarm."

Thankfully, there were only a handful of people still on board. Phoenix hurried back to Boomer.

"Where is it?"

"Halfway down, five feet in, attached to the support beam. You can't miss it, it's covered in duct tape."

Boomer descended the ladder, his mouth pinched in a thin line.

"I see it," he called, once he was in position. "I'm going to take a closer look."

Phoenix made to follow him. "I'll come with you. You might need my help."

Boomer held up a hand. "No. Let me take a look first. Stand by. I'll holler if I need you."

Phoenix didn't like it, but he nodded. Boomer was the expert.

Above them, staff members began to appear on deck, preparing for evacuation. "Take the second inflatable," Phoenix ordered. It was already tethered to the landing dock and was big enough to carry the remaining seven or eight people on board. They'd used it earlier to get underneath the other side of the rig. "Launching the lifeboat will take too long." He didn't know how much time they had.

Then, he heard the words he'd dreaded.

"It's counting down. Less than two minutes." Boomer's voice was quiet, but Phoenix could hear the finality in it. There wasn't enough time to defuse it.

Shit.

Phoenix yelled to Billy in the inflatable. "Go, now! Get away from the rig."

With a startled look, the roughneck jumped in and the cast off, bobbing away from the structure.

Phoenix yelled out to Boomer. "Get off there, buddy. Now!"

"I'm just going to try—"

"Now!" Phoenix shouted.

But he was too late.

The world exploded in a massive fireball, the shockwave slamming into him like a freight train. He was hurled off the ladder, the sea rushing up to meet him. Pain exploded through his body as he hit the water, darkness closing in around him, and then... nothing.

CHAPTER 19

*E*llie was a mile out when she saw the explosion. At first, she thought she was imagining things, but when thick black smoke began billowing into the sky, she panicked, her blood running cold.

Oh, my God!

Was that for real?

She floored the tiller, coaxing every last ounce of strength from the outboard motor, her heart racing with disbelief. What had happened? Had they hit gas? Had a pressure gauge blown? More importantly, was anyone hurt?

From out here, it looked like a massive explosion. Great big clouds of black smoke were unfurling into the air like some monstrous beast.

Shit. Shit. Shit.

In a blind panic, she gripped the tiller, anguished tears running down her face. As she sped towards the inferno, she could only pray everyone was alright.

Phoenix? Boomer? Billy?

Suzi would have left by now, along with most of the other

weekly workers, thank goodness, but what about the rest of the staff?

As she got nearer, she noticed another boat speeding away from the wreckage through the thick curtain of smoke. Black, sleek, and going at one hell of a pace, she hadn't noticed it before. It didn't look like one of the boats attached to the Explorer.

By the time she reached the burning jack-up rig, the black boat had disappeared into the distance, lost in the smoke. She slowed and gazed in horror at the debris floating around the base of the rig. An enormous, jagged gash had been blown through the center, the steel innards—pipes and wires—hanging down like garish metal entrails.

Cutting the engine, she bobbed amongst the flotsam, desperately searching for signs of life.

"Phoenix!" Her voice sounded hollow and insignificant amidst the backdrop of the raging inferno consuming the rig. "Boomer!" She couldn't see any bodies, but that didn't mean there weren't any.

Oh God, please let them be alive...

Tears poured down her face, making it hard to see through the stinging smoke. The rig burned ferociously, the searing heat scorching her skin even at this distance. The launch pad had disintegrated, and the great jack-up rig groaned mournfully as its twisted steel structure listed heavily to one side like a wounded beast.

How could this happen?

What should she do? With violently shaking hands, she managed to pull out her phone. No reception. That wasn't surprising since they relied on the Wi-Fi on the rig to communicate with the outside world. Fat lot of good that was now—it had all been blown to smithereens along with the rest of the structure. She should have brought a sat phone with her...

A short, anguished cry cut through the smoke, and she turned to see the second inflatable bobbing a few hundred yards away, having been hidden behind the remnants of the scorched rig.

"Oh, thank God!" She headed toward it.

Billy stood at the helm, frantically beckoning to her, his face a mask of shock. "Holy shit, Ellie. We just got off the damn thing in time."

"What happened?" She stared at him, wide-eyed, her mind reeling. He looked haggard, his face pinched and strained, as if he'd aged a decade in minutes.

"Phoenix found an explosive device of some sort under the rig. Boomer was checking it out when it detonated. They gave us a warning, and we got everyone into the boat. Not a second too soon." He coughed and raked a trembling hand through his hair, his eyes haunted.

Her voice was a hoarse, choked whisper. "What about Phoenix and Boomer? Where are they?"

He shook his head, his expression grim.

A wrenching sob caught in her throat as icy realization crashed over her.

"I'm sorry. I don't think they made it."

Please, no.

"We didn't even have time to get a mayday out. Nobody knows what's happened."

"I saw a boat speeding away from the rig as I was coming in," she said, her voice sounding hollow and distant to her own ears. How could Phoenix and Boomer be dead? It wasn't possible. Men like them didn't just die.

No, it couldn't be true. She refused to believe it.

"Really?" Billy seemed confused, his brow furrowing. "I didn't see anyone leave."

She shook her head, too stunned to continue, grief and

shock numbing her senses. Maybe she'd imagined it? None of this felt real.

"There's another exploratory rig, the Discoverer, fifteen miles out," she told him, forcing herself to focus. "Have you got enough gas to get there?"

He nodded jerkily. "Yeah. I think so."

She gave him the coordinates, her voice sounding like someone else's. "Get the remaining crew over there then call for help."

"What about you?"

"I'm going to stay here and keep searching. They might still be alive." Even saying the words aloud felt like a foolish, desperate fancy, but she clung to that faint shred of hope like a lifeline.

He gave a somber nod, but she could tell by the grim set of his face that he thought that tragically unlikely. Still, she had to try. She couldn't rest until she'd seen their bodies with her own eyes.

If there was even the slightest chance...

She swallowed hard over the painful lump in her throat. "Send help, Billy. Go. Now."

He gave a last nod, turned the lifeboat in the direction she'd given him, then set off, the engine sputtering to life. She watched it chug slowly away until it faded into the billowing smoke.

Alone, her tears came in earnest. Great, wracking sobs that shook her entire body as the horrible reality sank in.

God, please don't let him be dead.

She couldn't believe it. *Wouldn't* believe it.

She drifted listlessly around the debris field, hot tears streaming down her cheeks. Every now and then she'd stop and call out his name. Boomer's name. But nothing. All she got in reply was the tortured groaning of the rig as it kept tilting to one side, and the smell of scorched metal.

What was that?

A faint tapping sound could be heard in the eerie silence.

She froze, listening hard, hardly daring to breathe. There it was again.

Tap-tap-tap. Taaap-taaap-taaap. Tap-tap-tap.

Was that an SOS? Or was her battered, shell-shocked mind playing tricks on her? Was it just the metallic death throes of the gutted rig as it sank slowly beneath the waves?

Ellie restarted the engine with fumbling fingers and moved warily in the direction of the tapping.

"Hello?" she yelled through the smog, her voice cracking. "Anybody there?"

Tap-tap-tap. Taaap-taaap-taaap. Tap-tap-tap.

That was definitely an SOS. Too rhythmic and regular to be caused by the remnants of the rig collapsing in on itself.

Then she saw him, and her heart seized in her chest.

He was lying in the water, clutching a plank of wood. He'd made the banging sound by tapping a piece of steel piping onto what was left of the base of the structure.

Phoenix!

"Oh, my God. You're alive!" She steered the inflatable boat toward him, then reached over and tried to haul him in. He was barely conscious. A deep gash in his hairline leaked blood over his face, and there was another on his arm.

Shit, how was she going to get him into the boat? He was heavy—a dead weight—and unable to help himself. She heaved with all her might until finally she had half of his bulk on the edge of the inflatable. With one last pull, she managed to tip him over the side, and he collapsed into the bottom of the boat.

She dropped to her knees beside him. "Are you alright? Phoenix, speak to me. Can you hear me?"

He tried to open his eyes, but when he did, she noticed

they were glazed and unfocused. He was concussed. How badly, she didn't know.

But at least he was alive.

"Where's Boomer?" she asked him, but he didn't respond. He passed out, and if it wasn't for his shallow breathing, she might have thought he was dead.

"Wake up." She gently shook his shoulders. "Please, Phoenix." She'd read somewhere that you shouldn't go to sleep with a concussion because you might never wake up. Whether it was true or not, she had no idea, but she thought she'd better try.

He didn't move.

"Don't die on me," she whispered, smoothing back the hair on his forehead and inspecting the gash. "Don't you dare die on me." It wasn't too deep, but there was swelling around it. That might be what was causing the concussion—or the blast from the explosion. Either way, he needed medical attention, and now.

She didn't have enough gas to reach the Discoverer, but Billy would send help as soon as he could. She estimated half an hour for him to make the journey, another half an hour for them to send a vessel to come and get them. After that, they'd send a rescue crew, the Coast Guard, and forensics from the mainland, but that would take much longer.

Ellie chugged around the base of the rig, looking for Boomer. If Phoenix had somehow managed to survive the blast, maybe he had too. But she couldn't see him in the water. He wasn't hanging on to the burning rig, either.

She took a shuddering gasp. He obviously hadn't made it.

Turning her attention back to Phoenix, she tried to make him more comfortable. "Help is on the way," she whispered. "Hang in there."

A low hum caught her attention. Looking up, she saw a

black dot coming toward her. Was the speedboat she'd seen earlier coming back?

Yes, it looked like it. Low, sleek, and black. It sped across the ocean, getting bigger as it came toward her.

Thank God. Help was coming.

Tears began to fall afresh. Phoenix was going to be okay.

CHAPTER 20

"Incoming!" yelled Viper, so named because he was lethal with an M110 sniper rifle. At over a thousand yards, there was nobody better. "Take cover!"

They ducked, seconds before a rocket-propelled grenade hit the bunker they were hiding out in. The force threw Phoenix back against the concrete wall, knocking the air from his lungs. The searing heat made his skin blister. He coughed and groaned, pain lancing through his skull.

"Phoenix? Phoenix, wake up!" urged a distant voice, garbled and indistinct. It wasn't anyone from his unit. It was Ellie.

"Ellie?" he mumbled, but the roaring flames were too intense, engulfing the bunker and driving out the oxygen. He struggled to breathe, his vision darkening at the edges.

"We've gotta get out of here," Viper yelled from somewhere far away. Strong hands grabbed Phoenix under his arms and lifted him up off the dirty floor. Grunting with effort, Viper dragged him out of the burning bunker and into the blinding daylight.

Phoenix shut his eyes against the piercing brightness that

sent stabs of agony through his head. The world spun violently. "Need... to... rest," he slurred, his words barely audible.

"Sorry, buddy. We've got to get you somewhere safe. We're under heavy fire here."

The distant rat-a-tat of machine gun fire echoed in Phoenix's ringing ears as Viper carried him across uneven desert ground pockmarked with dry bushes and shrubs. They skidded to a halt behind a small rise where there was a modicum of cover. Here Viper laid him down, but Phoenix barely felt it, drifting in and out of awareness. His head throbbed mercilessly, feeling like it would split open. Why was everything so bright?

He tried to open his eyes but saw only blurry, disjointed images—Viper laying down covering fire, another guy chucking grenades like he was in a school food fight. Nothing made sense.

"Duck!" yelled Viper as another explosion rocked the ground nearby. Fragments of dust flew into the air then coated them in a fine, yellow mist.

Phoenix coughed weakly, every breath sending sharp pains through his ribs. He forced his eyes open again to find Viper had been replaced by Ellie, her long brown hair shot through with gold in the sunlight. She was so beautiful. He reached out a trembling hand to touch her, to make sure she was real, but she seemed to slip away into the haze.

"Ellie?" he croaked, his voice ragged.

"Oh, thank God you're awake." Her words sounded muffled, as if underwater. "Don't worry, help is on the way."

He tried to sit up, but his head exploded in blinding agony and he collapsed back, darkness threatening to pull him under again. Where was he? The rocking motion beneath him suggested a boat. But what was Ellie doing driving it? And where was the rig?

Fragmented memories slowly surfaced through the fog in his brain. The IED. The deafening explosion. The shock of cool water closing over his head.

"Boomer?" Phoenix choked out, forcing himself into a half-sitting position despite the waves of dizziness and nausea.

Ellie shook her head, her face blurring in and out of focus. "I'm sorry. He didn't make it." Her voice cracked with a strangled sob, then she took a shuddering breath as if barely keeping it together. "The others got away on the second inflatable, but I couldn't find Boomer anywhere..." More broken sobs escaped her. The boat jerked unsteadily as she fought to control her emotions.

"What?" The news hit Phoenix like a physical blow. She was fading in and out of his vision now, surrounded by sparkling spots and stars. He recognized the signs of a severe concussion, his brain struggling to process what he'd just heard. Boomer was dead?

The world tilted and spun sickeningly. Phoenix gripped the side of the boat, fighting a powerful wave of nausea. He leaned over and retched, but nothing came up except bitter saliva.

Ellie's hand gripped his shoulder, anchoring him. "Are you okay? You were nearly blown up. There's a deep gash on your head. I think you have a serious concussion."

"I've had worse," Phoenix mumbled, but a small, distant part of him knew that wasn't true. He'd never felt so disoriented, so untethered from reality.

"Here comes a rescue boat." Ellie's voice broke through the mental fog, laced with tentative hope as she nodded towards the horizon.

He stared in that direction, willing his eyes to focus, but all he could see was a blurry, undulating line of blue. "You sure?"

"Yes, can't you see it?" She pointed into the distance. "Over there."

Shielding his sensitive eyes against the intense sunlight with an unsteady hand, Phoenix squinted at the horizon. He knew from experience that the disorientation and light sensitivity would fade in a few hours, assuming there was no internal bleeding. He just had to hold on until then.

Gradually, a dark shape materialized in the distance. He stared at it, unblinking, as it slowly sharpened into the silhouette of an approaching boat. But something about it felt off, warning bells sounding dimly in the back of his muddled mind. His instincts, honed by years in the elite naval unit, whispered that this was no rescue vessel.

"It's going too fast," he said faintly, the words slurring together.

"What? It's coming to see if anyone needs rescuing."

He shook his head and instantly regretted it as the world lurched sickeningly. Swallowing hard against the rising bile, he fought to string the words together. "No, she's riding too high, moving too fast."

He sensed Ellie's hand tighten on the tiller, the boat's speed decreasing fractionally. "What are you saying, Phoenix?" Fear crept into her tone.

The mystery boat was about seven hundred yards away now and closing fast. Phoenix strained to make out the figures on board, but they remained frustratingly blurry, wavering in and out of focus.

"Anyone else onboard?" he asked, relying on Ellie to be his eyes.

She peered at the approaching craft. "Yes, I can see two men. They're both standing at the helm."

"Two men, for a rescue? I don't think so."

"They could've been nearby and saw the explosion," Ellie

suggested, but doubt colored her words. "There might be more in the back that I can't see."

It was possible, but the way the boat raced towards them, a predator scenting blood, made Phoenix's gut tighten with certainty. This was no rescue party.

"Turn around," he instructed, forcing the words out past gritted teeth.

"What?" Confusion and fear battled in Ellie's eyes.

"Turn around," Phoenix repeated urgently, his voice rough with pain but steeled with grim determination. "We need to get out of here. Now."

"But they've already seen us," Ellie protested weakly. "And we don't have enough fuel to go far."

Phoenix locked eyes with her, his gaze intense despite the foggy double-vision. "Doesn't matter. Just turn us around. Hurry."

With hesitant, jerky movements, Ellie spun the inflatable into a wide 180-degree turn. The mystery boat was faster and more maneuverable, but there was still a quarter mile of open ocean between them. A slim lead, but it would have to be enough.

Phoenix slumped back, fighting to stay conscious as pain pounded through his abused skull. "Floor it," he managed through clenched teeth, praying they could outrun whoever was on their tail. "Get us out of here."

The little dinghy shot forward, its hull rising out of the water as it gathered speed, then lowered as they opened up again. The wind whipped up their hair, and Phoenix fell against the side of the boat, feeling like a herd of elephants was parading around inside his skull. "Keep going and don't stop until I tell you," he managed through gritted teeth.

"Who are they?" Ellie asked, a tinge of hysteria in her voice.

"I'm not sure, but that's not a rescue boat."

"Why would they want to harm us? Surely, they're here to help?"

"I don't know, Ellie, but you have to trust me on this."

He could hear the uncertainty in her voice, but she didn't slow down.

A loud bang rang out, like a firecracker. "Get down!" Phoenix yelled, reacting instinctively despite the pain lancing through his head.

Ellie ducked, her eyes wide with disbelief. "Are... Are they shooting at us?"

More shots rang out, the sound echoing across the water.

"Just stay down and keep going!" Phoenix shouted, fighting to stay conscious as the world tilted and spun around him.

"Oh, my God." Ellie's voice was almost hysterical. "Why are they shooting at us?"

Phoenix couldn't answer that. He could only pray they had enough time to outrun the hostile vessel, or that it would redirect to the site of the explosion to scavenge off the doomed oil rig.

Risking a peek over the side, he saw the speedboat gaining on them, only four hundred yards away now.

More shots were fired, the distinctive rattle of automatic weapons sending a chill down Phoenix's spine. This wasn't good.

"Keep going," he shouted at Ellie, who had gone white with fear. She huddled down in front of the outboard motor, both hands clutching the tiller in a death grip. Despite the terror etched on her face, Phoenix was impressed at how she'd managed to keep it together. He'd seen civilians panic under far less provocation.

Three hundred yards.

Bullets whizzed through the air and fizzled into the sea around them, kicking up small geysers of spray. Thankfully, it was hard, if not impossible, to hit a fast-moving target, especially one bobbing up and down as well as surging forward, from a speeding boat. Phoenix knew this from experience, having tried it several times himself. As long as they maintained some distance, they should be okay for a little while longer. But he also knew something had to give. Eventually, the pursuing speedboat would catch up to them, and then it was game over.

Phoenix's mind raced, desperately searching for a way out of this nightmare, but the pounding in his head made it hard to think. Black spots danced at the edges of his vision, threatening to pull him back into the void. He blinked hard, fighting to stay awake, to stay focused. Ellie needed him. He couldn't pass out now.

The roar of the speedboat's engine grew louder, like an angry hornet's nest. Phoenix risked another glance back, squinting against the glare of the sun on the water. The gap had closed to two hundred yards, the figures on board now clearly visible. Two men, both armed, their faces obscured by dark sunglasses.

Phoenix's heart sank. These were no amateurs out for a joyride. They had the look of trained professionals, the kind who wouldn't stop until they finished the job.

Another burst of gunfire ripped through the air, the bullets zipping past so close Phoenix could almost feel their heat. Ellie screamed, the sound piercing through the fog in his brain. He had to do something, and fast, or they were both dead.

CHAPTER 21

"What are you doing?" Ellie asked, as the speedboat gained on them.

Phoenix didn't reply. He just leaned forward and rustled in the storage compartment, his movements clumsy and uncoordinated.

"Ah-ha!" He sat upright, clutching something in his hand. "A flare gun."

"So what?" What use was a flare gun against automatic firepower? When the Coast Guard got here, they could use it to signal their position, if they were still alive.

Phoenix seemed to be having trouble focusing, his eyes squinting as he tried to position himself in a lying position facing the pursuing vessel.

Two hundred yards.

"They're gaining on us." She was unable to keep her voice from shaking. "Oh, God. Phoenix, they're going to catch us."

"Don't worry. You just focus on keeping the inflatable moving forward. Leave them up to me," he said, his words slightly slurred.

She stared at him, concerned by his unsteady movements and labored breathing. Gone was the confident private security operative, replaced by a man clearly struggling with the effects of his concussion. How on earth was he going to take care of them with a flare gun when the bad guys were raining bullets on their heads?

"Steady..." he urged, his voice strained. "I've only got one shot at this."

His body swayed, his hands shaking as he tried to grip the flare gun and point it at the pursuers.

This wasn't looking good. Still, he was right. This was their one shot.

Ellie held her breath, her hands tightening on the tiller. Phoenix pulled the trigger. The canister shot out of the muzzle, flew across the water like a wobbly torpedo, and hit the vessel pursuing them just off-center of the windshield. It exploded into a Catherine wheel of sparks, causing both men to hit the deck and the boat to veer off course. Because it was going so fast, it lurched dangerously before the engine faltered, and it drifted to a halt.

"Yes!" Ellie stared at him. "You did it!"

"It'll buy us some time," he said, his voice weak. "Those guys will be suffering from burns and possibly blunt force trauma from the impact. They won't be going anywhere but to the hospital."

"I had no idea flares were so dangerous," Ellie mused. She felt like hugging Phoenix, she was so relieved, but he was clearly in no shape for any kind of physical contact. How he'd managed to aim well enough to hit the boat, she had no idea. But he had, and they were safe—for now.

"We've got to put some distance between us and them. Where's the nearest island?"

Ellie retrieved her GPS. "Here, let me look," she said, not

even bothering to pass it to him. Right now, she didn't even know which direction they were heading in. The only thing on her mind had been to get away from their attackers as fast as possible. She squinted into the distance. Nothing. Not a hazy mountain, a ship, or even a palm tree. The smoke from the oil rig had made everything hazy, so it was difficult to see what was out there.

Ellie took her time with the GPS, studying their location and the surrounding area. "There is a small island about four miles north of our current location. It looks like a protected nature reserve."

"Perfect, we'll head there," Phoenix said.

She glanced doubtfully at the fuel tank. "I don't know if we're going to make it."

He gave her a thin smile. "We don't have much choice."

There was a silence, then Phoenix said quietly, "Did you see Boomer's body?"

A lump formed in her throat. "No, I didn't. Do you think he could have survived the blast?"

Phoenix shook his head, then winced. "No, he was disarming the IED when it went off. He would have gotten the brunt of it."

"God, I'm so sorry," Ellie whispered.

"Yeah, I spotted it climbing back onto the rig. It was strapped underneath the platform." He paused, his eyes drifting shut for a moment before he forced them open again. "It was triggered remotely, Ellie, by someone onboard that rig or within Wi-Fi distance."

"But who could it have been?" she whispered. "Most of the staff took the chopper back to the mainland."

"I don't know. They could have come back to the rig—" he petered off with a shrug, then grimaced, reaching for his head.

Ellie gasped. "I saw a speedboat when I was coming back from the Discoverer."

"You did?" Phoenix asked, his words coming slowly as if he was having trouble processing the information.

She nodded, her eyes wide. "That must have been the bomber."

Phoenix confirmed it, his voice strained. "That would have been our perp, all right. The timing fits. Did you see who it was?"

"No." If only she had taken more notice. "The sun was too bright, and I was too far away. It was only one person, though."

Phoenix grimaced, his eyes closing again. "Was it the one following us?"

"It could have been." She bit her lip. "I don't really know. The speedboat chasing us had two men on board though, not one."

"He could have picked someone up. Maybe there's a control boat nearby. A yacht."

Ellie nodded. It was possible, although she hadn't seen anything.

"This is because of me, isn't it?" she whimpered.

Phoenix opened his eyes. They were still glassy and unfocused. "No, it's because of what you discovered. Someone is trying to prevent it from getting out."

"But why?" Ellie asked, her mind racing. "Why would anyone want Xonex to think they'd found a major oil deposit if it wasn't true?"

Phoenix took a deep breath, wincing as he did so. "Think about it. If Xonex believed they were on the verge of a big discovery, what would happen to their stock price?"

Ellie suddenly saw where he was going. "It would soar."

"Exactly. And if someone knew the truth, they could buy a ton of shares before the announcement and then sell them off at the peak, making a fortune."

"Insider trading," Ellie murmured.

"On a massive scale," Phoenix agreed. "But there is another possibility."

"What?"

"It could be a rival company. Maybe they're trying to sabotage Xonex, making them pour resources into a dead end. It would cripple them financially."

"The survey company must be involved," Ellie concluded. "That's how all this started."

Phoenix nodded. "For sure, but I doubt they were acting alone. They'd have been paid by someone to create the false reports. It might even be a mole within Xonex."

"Industrial sabotage." Ellie shook her head. "I can't believe this."

"Whatever the reason, they're desperate to keep the truth from getting out."

Ellie looked out at the vast expanse of ocean, suddenly feeling very small and very vulnerable. "So what do we do now?"

Phoenix turned around, his movements clumsy. "Our first and only priority is to get to that island. When we are safe, we can contact the Coast Guard and let them know where we are."

"Okay." Ellie was glad they finally had a plan. She looked down and saw that her feet were wet. Water was slopping over them, pooling at her side of the inflatable. "Um, Phoenix. We're taking on water."

He frowned. "One of their bullets must have hit the inflatable."

Ellie's heart sank. "Now what?"

"See if you can find the hole." His words tumbled out, all

running together. "I'll take the tiller. We need to plug it up if we have any hope of making it to the island."

Oh, God. They were going to die. The inflatable would sink, and they'd drown out here, in the middle of nowhere. Ellie tried to focus on her breathing, but the fear kept rising.

"Ellie."

She began gasping for air.

"Ellie, look at me."

She turned her head, and focused on his chiseled face, his eyes hazy but still a deep, cobalt blue. "I need you, Ellie. Don't fall apart on me now. I can't do this on my own. You have to keep it together."

She knew he was right. With a concussion, he wouldn't be much use. She couldn't freak out now.

I need you.

"I'll try."

Concentrate on what he'd said. Find the hole.

She scrambled around the rigid bottom of the boat on her hands and knees, looking for the leak. She felt an area where the water was colder than anywhere else. There was also a gentle pressure against her fingertips under one of the two lightweight aluminum seats that spanned the width of the boat. "Got it!"

"How big is it?"

She traced the bullet hole with her finger. Water was streaming in. "It's pretty big. I don't think we can plug it."

His expression hardened. "Then we have a problem."

They *were* going to die. She knew it.

He squinted into the distance. "How far is that island?"

Holy crap. He wasn't suggesting—

"It's too far to swim," she said, reading his thoughts.

"Get the life jackets."

Oh, God.

With shaking hands, she rifled in the compartment then

pulled out two orange life vests. He kept the boat aimed at the island. "With a bit of luck, we'll get there before we take on too much water."

At that moment, the outboard motor coughed, spluttered, then died.

CHAPTER 22

They were adrift a mile from land. Phoenix checked the fuel tank—it was dry. And there was no reserve canister.

Damnit.

He slammed his hand down on the empty tank in frustration.

"What are we going to do?" Ellie asked, her eyes huge. He could tell she was still on the verge of having another panic attack, but so far, she was managing to keep it at bay.

Time to get specific. He tried to clear the fogginess and think. "How good a swimmer are you?"

"I'm okay," she replied, her eyes on the looming shape of the island. "But I won't make a mile in open water."

"It's more like three quarters of a mile now."

She just stared at him.

"I could swim and pull the boat," he offered.

She shot him an incredulous look. "You're injured. You've got a concussion and a three-inch gash in your arm that needs stitches."

He glanced at the bandage she'd wrapped around his

wound. That was the least of his worries. His concern was his still-pounding head, though it didn't hurt quite as bad as before. The nausea had subsided too. That was a good sign. "It's either that or we both swim for it."

Most people he knew would opt for being pulled. It was a far easier ride, but not Ellie. She stared at him for a long time, then fastened her life jacket. "Let's swim. You'll never make it by pulling the boat."

He gave a tight nod, touched by her thoughtfulness.

Plus, they'd get there faster, and then they could find a ranger's station and radio for help. It would be dark in a couple of hours, and he didn't fancy traipsing through the jungle at night. These barrier islands were fairly tropical, with some dangerous creatures lurking in the rivers and bushes. He didn't tell her that, however. No need to freak her out more than she already was.

Phoenix checked what little equipment he had on him. He was still wearing his board shorts but no T-shirt. He hadn't had time to put one on before the explosion. His hunting knife was secured snugly in the pocket of his shorts —thank God. That would come in handy on the island. They could use it to hunt for food, if necessary. Or as a weapon.

It wouldn't be too long before those idiots in the speedboat radioed back to their bosses and another craft got underway. Hopefully, they'd find the empty inflatable and assume he and Ellie had drowned, but he knew that was overly optimistic. If they were the type of men he thought they were—hired mercenaries—they wouldn't want any survivors.

He was pretty sure they'd send more men after them. It was just a matter of time.

Phoenix had spent half his SEAL training in the water, so he wasn't concerned about the one-mile swim. He could make three or four times that distance easily, even with a concussion. It was Ellie he was worried about.

She said she could swim, but he only had her word for it. As Phoenix checked her life vest, he said, "If you run into trouble, just float on your back."

Eyes huge, she nodded up at him. She was being so incredibly brave right now. His heart swelled with pride, and he resisted the urge to take her into his arms. She was putting her life at risk for him, because he had a concussion.

"You're sure about this, Ellie. I don't mind—"

"I'm sure. Let's go." She turned to face the water. The inflatable was sinking fast, deflating like a child's pool toy. They had maybe ten minutes left, before it wouldn't support their weight anymore.

"Give me your shoes," he said.

"Huh?" She spun back around.

"Just do it. You'll need them on the island, but you can't swim in them."

"Oh, okay." She bent down and took them off.

Phoenix kicked off his, tied all the laces together, then fastened them to the string on his shorts. "Ready?"

Ellie took a deep breath, then nodded.

"We're going to be fine." He touched her cheek. He wanted nothing more than to hold her and shield her from all of this.

"I hope you're right," she whispered back.

"I'll make sure of it. "

Phoenix fastened his own life jacket, then sat on the edge and fell backwards into the water.

Re-emerging, he waited while she did the same. "Come on, let's go."

They swam slowly, but steadily, toward the island. Ellie was pretty good. With the buoyancy aid, she'd have no trouble reaching the shore.

"You're doing great," he encouraged, ignoring the pain in

his head and the sting in his arm. Pride surged through him at her determined strokes.

The water was calm thanks to the light wind blowing onshore. That would make it easier. Once he'd had to swim five miles through the choppy Atlantic with all his gear during a training exercise off the Virginia coast. This was a breeze compared to that.

"How is your head?" she called, after they'd been swimming for about ten minutes.

"Fine," he lied. It was back to throbbing, thanks to the exertion, but he liked the water, and the rhythmic strokes relaxed him. Usually, he could continue in this vein for hours, once he got into the zone.

They carried on. At first, it appeared like the island wasn't getting any closer, but as they persevered, the outline became bigger. When they were roughly five hundred yards out, the sea suddenly got choppier and the breeze heavier.

"There's a reef out here," he called, treading water while he waited for Ellie to catch up. "It might get a bit rough, but once we get over it, it'll be nice and calm."

"Okay." She was panting, her breath coming in heavy gasps, but she hadn't complained once. His breath caught in his throat as he thought about the men after them. He'd do his utmost to keep her safe. The need to protect this incredible woman overwhelmed him.

"How much further?" she asked, once she'd caught her breath.

He squinted at the landmass in front of them. "We're nearly there. You're doing great."

Half a mile might not sound like a lot, but when you're in the water, it can feel never-ending. Every stroke depletes your energy; every muscle in your body is working at the same time, trying to keep you afloat, propel you forward, and keep your body temperature normal. That's why swimmers were some of the fittest athletes around.

"What was that?" Ellie barked suddenly.

"What?" Phoenix glanced around, but he couldn't see anything. Dread knotted his stomach.

"Shit, Phoenix, I thought I saw something. A shadow beneath us." Her voice was higher pitched than normal, a sure sign of anxiety.

"It's probably just a large fish." He kept his voice calm. "They grow pretty big around the reefs." On cue, a steel-gray fin broke the surface about fifteen feet in front of them.

"Holy crap, Phoenix," Ellie cried. "It's a shark."

Fucking hell. Could this day get any worse?

Still, a shark was nothing to panic about. Not yet.

He glanced at his injured arm. It was still bandaged tightly, but there was a faint red smudge on the surface. The shark was probably smelling the blood. "It's me." He raised his injured arm out of the water.

"W—What are we going to do?" She was shivering with fear. Her huge eyes followed the jagged fin as it circled them. Generally speaking, if a shark was visible, it wasn't planning to attack. In the vast majority of fatal shark attacks, the victim didn't see the shark coming. It attacked from below, surprising its prey.

"Nothing. You're going to keep swimming. Head towards the reef. Once you're over that, it'll be fine. Sharks don't enter the bay because they sense they can't get out again. It's a defense mechanism."

"B—But what about you?" He loved that she cared. His heart clenched.

"I'm going to use the plastic wrapping around the GPS to cover my wound. That way the shark won't smell the blood. Then, I'm going to follow you." His voice was calmer than he felt. He'd die before he let anything happen to her.

"Will that work?" she sounded doubtful.

"Yeah, but it'll mean we lose the GPS." That would be a shame. They could have used it on the island, but there were other ways of locating the ranger's office.

"Just do it," urged Ellie, still treading water. "Do you need my help?"

"No, I'm good. You keep going."

She hesitated, then swam up to him. "I know you're looking out for me, but it'll be quicker if I help you."

His heart skipped a beat. "Okay, thanks." She was right. Fixing his arm one-handed was awkward and he didn't want to hang around here longer than necessary. He handed her the GPS, keeping an eye on the fin. Tiger shark, he guessed. They were the most common out here on the reefs. Also the most temperamental.

Ellie unwrapped the GPS. The plastic covering was the kind used to wrap sandwiches. It would do perfectly for the wound, except it was wet. "You'll have to tie it off," he said. "It won't stick."

She wrapped it around his bandage several times. "That's not too tight, is it?"

"It's perfect."

She tied the two ends together as firmly as she could. "There."

"Okay, let's go." The longer they stayed out here, the higher the risk of an attack.

Slowly but steadily, they swam in the direction of the reef. The shark didn't follow.

Thank God.

He could handle most things, but a tiger shark was not one of them.

As they got nearer, the water bubbled like a cauldron over the ragged and uneven coral. Foamy waves and crests sprung up, slapping them in the face and obscuring their vision. He used his upper body strength to keep his head above water, conscious that Ellie wouldn't be able to do the same. The closer they got, the wilder and more chaotic the waves. Soon they were breaking over his head, the salt stinging his eyes.

"You okay?" he shouted to Ellie, who was a few yards behind him.

To his relief, he heard a garbled, "Yeah".

"Only a few more yards. Keep going."

She didn't reply—too busy keeping her head above the rampaging white water, determination etched her face.

His heart swelled. Damn, she was something else. It was then that he decided. If they made it out of this alive, he was never letting her go.

CHAPTER 23

*E*llie forced her leaden arms to keep moving. Thank heavens for the buoyancy aid. Without it, she'd never have made it this far. When there was a lull in the waves, she could see the calm, mirror-like surface of the bay beyond.

Come on, keep swimming.

One last kick through a frenzied peak and trough, choking on a mouthful of salty seawater—and she was over the worst. The water stilled, the reef beneath them disappeared, replaced by the sandy bottom. It was like swimming through a lagoon.

Catching her breath, Ellie turned onto her back and floated for a while. The sky was a cloudless blue, the color of Phoenix's eyes.

They'd made it.

Ellie felt a squishy thing touch her leg, then a jolt of pain spread through her limbs.

"Ouch," she yelped.

Her first thought was the shark, but when she looked

down, she realized it wouldn't be. Phoenix had said they didn't venture over the jagged reef.

"You okay?" He swam up beside her.

"Something stung me." She bit her lip against the pain. Damn, just as she'd been enjoying their victory.

"Don't worry. It's probably a jellyfish, but they aren't poisonous. They'll just give you a nasty rash."

Phew! That was a relief, although a rash didn't sound good.

On any other day she'd have panicked at the thought of being stung by a jellyfish, but after being shot at, sinking, and almost being attacked by a shark—it somehow didn't feel that bad. She nearly laughed at the thought. How far she'd come from that fearful, anxious woman he'd tackled on her first day on the rig.

"Are you able to swim?"

"Yeah, I think so." Her leg ached, but it seemed localized, and her other limbs were working fine. Phoenix switched to a leisurely breaststroke. A strong swimmer, he seemed so at ease in the water. Ellie glanced across at him. "Did you do a lot of this type of thing in the Navy?"

He gave that secretive smile. "All the time."

"So, this is just another day at the office for you?"

A dry chuckle. "Not quite. I've never been that close to an IED before, or come face to face with a tiger shark, but don't worry. I won't let anything happen to you."

She managed a weak smile. "I know you won't."

His expression softened, but then he turned away and nodded toward the crescent strip of sand ahead. "We're there."

They clambered out of the lagoon onto the finest, softest sand Ellie had ever felt. She collapsed, spent, and lay on her back enjoying the warmth and the stability of being on dry land. Apart from the sting on her leg, she felt like she could lie here, perfectly content, forever. "I can't believe we made it."

He lay down beside her and squeezed his eyes shut. "I knew we could do it."

What he meant was, he knew *she* could do it. His faith in her was astounding. A week ago she wouldn't have believed she'd been capable of this. "How's your head?"

"Okay." He forced a smile, but she didn't miss the tension in his jaw or the deep crease in his forehead. He was in pain but wasn't telling her.

"Can we rest here for a while?" she asked, unclipping her life vest and slipping it off. "I don't think I can go any further right now."

"Sure." He sounded relieved. She lay her head back in the warm sand, while he took off his vest and did the same.

They lay in an exhausted silence for a while, listening to the waves crashing on the distant reef, the whispering palm trees, and the seagulls as they flew overhead. It was kind of idyllic. Under different circumstances, this would be a beautiful place to take a vacation or explore on a day off. Now they were here, being chased by men who wanted to kill them.

"I think Henderson is involved," she said softly, once she'd regained some of her strength.

He glanced over at her. "What makes you say that?"

"He hired me," she admitted, still feeling the crushing embarrassment of being played. "I think he did so expecting me to be too young and inexperienced to lead this project."

"You're perfectly capable—" Phoenix said.

"No, I'm really not. My only other role on a rig has been as part of a large team. I thought it was strange at the time, but it was good for my career, so I jumped at the chance." She bit her lip. "Meanwhile, he was using me because he thought I'd do my job and not ask too many questions. A more experienced engineer would have realized something was off with the survey reports long before I did."

Phoenix was silent for a moment, processing what she'd said. "Do you think he was the one who cut the railing, and tried to harm you during the storm?"

"It's possible. I've been thinking about it a lot, and he could have staged the accident to get me and Suzi up on deck. It was right after I'd voiced my concerns to him."

Phoenix shook his head angrily. The violent spark in his gaze made her catch her breath. He looked so dangerous in that moment, so lethal, with his granite expression and menacing stillness. She almost felt sorry for Henderson. Almost, but not quite.

"He may have set off the IED," Phoenix muttered. "Could it have been him you saw in the speedboat?"

"It could be, yeah. The man I saw had a similar height and build, now that you mention it."

"I think I know what happened." Phoenix's whole body bristled. "Henderson detonated the bomb, hoping to take out the rig, then he sped off to a waiting yacht when he saw you coming back. He informed the people he's working for, and they ordered two hired mercs to come after us. I'll bet they were there to tie up any loose ends."

"That's terrible," Ellie whispered, shocked at the extent of the scam. "What about the survivors? Do you think they made it to the Discoverer?"

He gave a grim nod. "I'm sure they did. We distracted the bad guys for long enough for Billy to get the others to safety."

"Thank goodness for that." She shivered, but not because she was cold. She couldn't believe someone would resort to such extreme measures for pure greed.

"When you're ready, we should try to find the ranger's station." Phoenix glanced up at the multicolored sky. The sun was setting, turning it into a rainbow of pinks, oranges and yellows. "It would be good to find shelter before it gets dark."

Ellie groaned and pushed herself up. Exhausted didn't even begin to cover it. Every tendon, every muscle in her body was aching. She wasn't even sure she could get to her feet.

"Let me take a look at your leg," he said, rising effortlessly. Even with a concussion, he was in better shape than she was.

His torso was pumped up from the swim, muscles bulging and rippling under tanned skin still glistening with saltwater. Years of intense training had sculpted his body into a work of art, all hard planes and ridges of muscle without an ounce of extra fat. His shoulders were broad, tapering down to a trim waist and abs you could grate cheese on. A trail of dark hair started below his navel and disappeared tantalizingly into the waistband of his shorts.

Ellie swallowed hard as he inspected her leg, her exhausted body suddenly flushing with heat that had nothing to do with the warm sand beneath them. She dragged her gaze back up to his face, trying to focus but finding it difficult. The man was built like a Greek god, for heaven's sake.

"Yep, that's a jellyfish sting. Is it very painful?"

"No," she said truthfully.

He smiled. "I've had plenty. I know it stings like hell."

She made to protest, but he held up a hand. "Don't move. I'll be right back."

"Wait! Where are you going?"

He disappeared into the bank of trees flanking the beach and was back before she had a chance to react. "Here, let's rub some of this on it."

She looked at the succulent green plant in his hand. "What's that?"

"Aloe vera. Its sap is brilliant for stings and bites. We often use it for bluebottle stings and the like in the Navy."

"Oh, I've heard of aloe vera before. I didn't know it grew here."

"It grows on most tropical beaches." He squeezed the juice onto her leg and rubbed it in. His fingers were gentle, caressing her leg like it was the most natural thing in the world. Then he stopped, but his fingers lingered.

The heat in his gaze was unmistakable. Ellie held her breath, unsure what was happening. She felt a deep connection to this man and wanted... Hell, she didn't know what she wanted and just stared at him, at a loss for how to deal with the yearning in her heart.

He cleared his throat. "That should help ease the pain and take some of the heat out of it."

"Thanks." Her skin prickled where he'd touched it, almost like he'd scorched it with his fingers.

A heavy pause stretched between them, the air electric.

"Ellie, I—" he didn't finish. Shaking his head, he made to move away.

She grabbed his arm. "Don't go just yet."

He hesitated but stayed where he was, with her hand wrapped around his forearm. She felt the muscle flex beneath his skin. Her heart pounded, threatened to jump right out of her chest, but she couldn't move. Not with his gaze, dark and questioning, locked on hers.

"Hold me," she whispered. She couldn't explain it, maybe it was the sheer exhaustion, or the realization that she'd nearly lost him today, but she needed to feel his arms around her, needed to know he was still there. "Please?"

Just for a moment, then they could go back to reality, to the explosion and the bad guys with guns chasing them.

Phoenix must have understood, because he nodded and enveloped her in his embrace, crushing her to him as if he'd never let her go. Closing her eyes, she absorbed his strength, his solidness, his body heat, letting all of it seep into her very bones. For the first time since she'd left the oil rig that morning, she felt truly safe. Wrapped in his arms was the only place she wanted to be. If only the world would disappear and leave them like this, cocooned in each other, forever.

"It's okay," he murmured against her ear, his voice husky and deep. "I've got you."

Tears welled, the sting of salt behind her lids, but she blinked them away. Now wasn't the time to give in to the emotion of the last few days, but damn, how she wanted to. If she'd been alone, she would have sobbed her heart out, but right now, she drew on his calm confidence and took some steadying breaths. She opened her eyes, met his gaze, and hoped he didn't see her longing.

"It's going to be okay. You know that, right?" He held her at arm's length. "I'm not going to let anything happen to you."

His words slayed her, piercing straight through to her battered heart. No one had ever said that to her before, let alone with such conviction, such unflinching certainty.

She believed him. She'd seen the rage in his eyes when she'd told him about Henderson. He would kill for her, she knew that. But she didn't know how to process it.

"I know," she whispered.

Slowly, he leaned in, his eyes dropping to her parted lips. Her breath hitched, her heart raced, as he drew closer, the heat of him searing her skin. She could feel his breath on her face, ragged and uneven.

She longed to kiss him, to be consumed by him, to have him chase away the ugliness, fear, and anxiety with the sheer force of his passion. Only he could do that for her. Only he could make her feel whole again.

She strained forward, her lips opening. His arms were still around her, holding her close against his broad chest. His heart beat fast and steady, in time with hers. But then he froze, his body going rigid.

Her eyes flew open, confused. What she saw in him made her catch her breath. Concern, mixed with something else, something she couldn't put her finger on. Was it fear? No. That wasn't it. Anger, maybe? Was he angry with her for reaching out, for needing him?

She swallowed and blinked as he pulled away, the loss of his touch a physical ache. The air began circulating between their bodies, cool and unwelcome.

With a flash of regret, he released her. "We should get going. It's getting dark."

The sun had set. She hadn't noticed.

Phoenix rose in one fluid motion, while she pushed herself to her hands and knees, unsure whether her legs would support her weight. They did, barely. He handed her shoes, his fingers brushing hers with a jolt of electricity. "You'd better put these on."

Wordlessly, she took them from him and slipped her feet into them. He did the same. Her head was swirling with need, embarrassment, regret.

"Ready?"

She nodded, aware he wasn't looking at her. His gaze was fixed on the line of trees up ahead, and the dark jungle beyond.

"Then let's go."

uck.

What was wrong with him? He'd had the woman he wanted more than anything in his arms, was seconds away from claiming her—and he'd frozen. Totally choked.

He'd seen the hurt in her eyes, the confusion. Damn, he felt like a jerk. Now she'd think he wasn't interested or she'd done something wrong, when in fact, it was he who had the problem.

He couldn't get over the feeling that she was too good for him. It was messed up. *He* was messed up. But after what she'd been through with that dickhead of an ex-boyfriend, he couldn't bring her into his world. His world was nothing but guilt and misery and frustration. Even with his new job at Blackthorn Security, he was still surrounded by the kind of life she despised.

Danger, violence, death.

He couldn't promise her anything. Nothing normal, anyway. Not security, not a stable income, not even a boyfriend who'd be around, because he wouldn't most of the time.

Ellie deserved more. So why did it hurt so goddamn much?

Hell, he wanted to devour her, consume her, show her how love should be. How a man should be. He wanted to eradicate her fear and replace it with passion. The need in her gaze had been so obvious, so addictive. Yet he'd turned her down.

What a moron! And so soon after he'd told himself he'd never let her go. Well, he hadn't. He'd pushed her away.

And now, in true Phoenix style, he was going to beat himself up about it. He turned to check she was okay, only to find her walking quietly behind him, eyes downcast, thoughts a million miles away. She was probably questioning what she'd ever seen in him—and he didn't blame her one little bit.

"Let's get beyond those dunes, where we'll be out of sight."

She didn't reply.

They walked across the long, wide beach strewn with driftwood and sea wrack. The sand was remarkably white and in the daytime would be almost blinding. Behind the beach were a series of undulating dunes, each topped with sea oats and marram grass swaying gently in the evening breeze. The dunes formed a natural barrier that protected the inner parts of the island, and it would also give them cover.

He didn't kid himself. They weren't home free. Those men meant business, and they'd be back. It was only a matter of time. The only hope he and Ellie had was reaching a ranger station and calling for assistance. They'd probably have to spend the night on the island, as no rescue boats would be launched until the morning. Hopefully, the guys pursuing them also wouldn't make it to the island until daylight. That way they'd have a good shot at being gone before trouble arrived.

They climbed the dunes, Ellie stumbling along next to him, her mouth set in a grim line. He offered her his hand, but she shook her head. "I'm okay."

They continued in silence, the squawking cries of seabirds filling the air. Every now and then he sensed her gaze on him, but she didn't speak, and he didn't know what to say to make it right. How could he tell her how much he cared? That he'd die before he let anything happen to her? That he admired her more than any other woman he'd ever met?

After his foolish behavior, would she even believe him?

Maybe it was for the best. If she thought he wasn't interested, that he didn't care, she wouldn't develop any feelings for him, or any she already had, would die if they hadn't already. There was no space for someone like her in his head, not beside his dead SEAL buddies and the guilt surrounding all of them.

They crested the dunes then slunk down the other side, their feet digging into the soft sand. Ellie stumbled, and he grabbed her arm, catching her before she fell. Her hands flew out, making contact with his bare chest. Her eyes locked on his, cautious, anxious. Hell, the last thing he wanted was her to be anxious. "You okay?"

"Yeah. Um, thanks."

He held her for a moment, savoring the feel of her. Her clothes had almost dried, but her hair was wild and disheveled, making him think of a forest nymph. Those huge tiger eyes were glowing softly in the dying light, filled with hopes and dreams he'd never discover. A physical pain hit him in the gut, and he winced.

Immediately, she frowned in concern. "Are you okay?"

"I'm fine." His voice was gruff, making her flinch.

She backed away from him and kept going down the dune, all practicality now, avoiding his gaze. They reached the bottom of the dune. The terrain now transitioned into a dense, lush coastal scrub thick with palmetto palms and twisted, gnarled trees that looked like they had weathered many storms.

A wooden sign, partially hidden by encroaching vegetation said, *Ranger Station*.

"That's it." He pointed to the sign.

She heaved a sigh of relief. "Thank goodness."

He peered through the brush. "Looks like some sort of trail."

Ellie nodded. "How far do you think it is?"

"Hard to say, but at least we know we're on the right track."

She nodded.

It was nearly dark now, and the air was filled with the rich, earthy aroma of salt and decay—a sharp contrast to the clean, briny smell of the sea. In the brush, it would be even darker. There were no footpaths that he could see, which meant traversing the uneven terrain in the dark and dealing with all the associated risks.

The temperature had dropped, and without his shirt, he was exposed to the mosquitoes and biting flies, not to mention scratches and scrapes by branches and leaves. They had maybe half an hour of dusk, then it would be pitch black. While he had some experience with jungle warfare, Ellie didn't, and he didn't want to frighten her more than necessary. She'd already been through a hell of an ordeal today.

They both had.

He kicked at pole with his foot, then wiggled it until it came lose.

"What are you doing?" Ellie asked.

"Confusing our enemies." He hauled it out of the damp ground and threw it into the dense brush, where it immediately got eaten up by foliage. "Come on, let's go." The longer they stood here, the darker it would get. "Stay close and move slowly. We'll follow the trail until we get to the ranger station. They'll have supplies there, and hopefully someone with a cell or sat phone."

She gave an eager nod. As they moved inland, the vegetation thickened and gave way to forest. He noticed Ellie give a little shiver and shuffle closer to him. It was dark and cool under the canopy. Phoenix was grateful for the isolation and the cover of darkness. It would make finding them so much harder, but he could tell Ellie was uneasy.

He proceeded slowly, but steadily, heading uphill. He calculated the highest point was probably about fifty to eighty feet above sea level, which meant they'd have to cover a distance of approximately three to five miles inland.

On average, humans walked at about three miles per hour on flat, easy terrain. However, since they were navigating through dense coastal scrub and forest without a footpath, their pace would slow to about two miles per hour. Covering a distance of three to five miles at two miles per hour would roughly take one-and-a-half to two-and-a-half hours.

Ellie stuck close to him, letting him hear her breath coming in shallow gasps. She was tiring, and walking uphill was taxing. They'd had no food, no water, and very little rest since the inflatable had sunk.

When the underbrush rustled, Ellie jumped. "What was that?"

"Probably a lizard or a shy snake," he said, trying not to frighten her. The forest floor was layered with fallen leaves, moss, and the occasional vine. Many that were still hanging smacked him in the chest or clung to his neck. He wished he had a machete to cut his way through, but this wasn't Belize, and he didn't have anything other than his trusty hunting knife, which wouldn't do shit against this type of foliage.

A short while later, he held up a hand. "Listen."

Ellie stopped, swaying slightly beside him. She needed a rest. "What?"

"Water." A soft tinkling sound could be heard echoing through the trees. "It's a river."

Ellie blinked at him, not understanding.

"Fresh water," he said. "We can rest there and regroup."

"Okay." A rushed whisper. She was close to collapse.

Taking her hand, he led her toward the sound until they came upon a small, clear freshwater stream. It seemed to gurgle up from a hidden underground spring then cascaded over the rocky bed, down toward the sea.

He lowered her onto a flat rock and gestured to the river. "Drink. We can rest here until you've got your strength back." A little groan told him she wasn't sure that was going to happen.

The freshwater tasted so good, and he drank his fill after Ellie. Then, he splashed his face, washing away the sweat. Finally, he took off the bandage to cleanse the cut on his arm. It looked red around the edges, and he worried it might be getting infected. Hopefully the ranger station would have a first-aid kit he could use.

"That looks bad," she said, sliding over.

"It'll be okay."

"You don't always have to be so brave," she said, quietly. "I mean, I appreciate the show of confidence, but it's okay to say you're tired or in pain."

"Really, I'm fine."

She sighed and asked for the second time. "How much farther?"

"Another hour, maybe."

"What if we can't find it?"

"Then we'll set up camp and wait until morning."

Another nod.

Phoenix hadn't been lying. His head was starting to ease, despite the gentle exercise, and he was feeling better than he had all day. His concussion must be lifting. Thank God it hadn't been too serious. Not like Boomer, who'd gotten the brunt of the blast. He hoped his friend had been rendered unconscious immediately and hadn't known what had hit him.

The thought sobered him, and after a short rest, he asked, "Are you okay to keep going?"

"I'll manage."

He admired her grit. Her face was pale in the light of the moon, shining down between the trees, and he'd never seen her look so wild.

After what felt like ages but was in fact a little under half an hour, the trees began to thin, and the ground sloped upward more steeply. "We must be close," he said.

Ellie sighed in relief.

They crested a small hill, and the ranger station finally came into view—a solitary, sturdy structure raised slightly off the ground on stilts to protect it from the damp ground. The exterior was weathered, its wooden, rustic appearance blending into the surrounding landscape.

"That's it."

"Thank God." Ellie rushed ahead, reaching the cabin before him. She tried the door, but it was locked. Not surprising, given the late hour. The cabin was in darkness, the lights off.

"It's closed." He heard the dejection in her voice, and his heart went out to her.

"Don't worry, we can still get in. We'll just have to make sure we vacate it before anyone arrives tomorrow." They needed medical supplies, food, and shelter—and it couldn't wait. His arm was beginning to throb, and they both had to eat something.

"But… how?"

"Give me a moment." Leaving Ellie standing at the front door, he circled the cabin, but there was no other entrance. No security cameras or flashing lights inside the property, which meant they probably didn't have an alarm. No need out here on the island. They had nothing worth stealing.

Bending down, he inspected the lock. It was an old-style mechanism that wouldn't be too hard to jimmy. After taking out his hunting knife, he wedged it into the gap then pried. The lock groaned before giving way.

They were in.

CHAPTER 25

*B*y the dim glow of the flickering lantern, Ellie watched Phoenix slide the heavy bolt in place and then pull a chest of drawers across the door. "That should do it," he said.

"Do you really think they're going to come for us here?" She couldn't hide the tremor from her voice. After the hike up to the summit, she just wanted to lie down and pass out. The thought of having to fight those two mercenaries, or whatever they were, filled her with dread.

"I hope not," was all he said, which did little to bolster her confidence. For the past half-hour, she had been resting inside while he set up what he called booby traps around the cabin's perimeter.

"An early warning system," he explained upon his return. "Just in case."

Then he set about checking the cabin. He opened all the cupboards and drawers, checked in every possible nook and cranny. One locked cabinet caught his eye, and using his knife, he forced it open.

"What are you looking for?" she asked.

"This." He turned around and held up a shotgun. "You never know, it might be useful."

"How'd you know that was in there?"

"I didn't, but it stands to reason that a ranger station like this would have a weapon on hand."

He thought of everything. At least now they were armed, and not just sitting ducks, should the men from the boat track them down.

"I found the first-aid kit." She pointed to the desk where she had placed it, alongside some bags of chips, cans of soda, and two chocolate bars. She had already devoured a bar and downed a soda before sinking into one of the chairs, utterly exhausted.

"Thanks." He lowered himself into the chair at the desk then opened the medical bag. The wound on his arm was still uncovered after he'd cleansed it in the stream, and it needed dressing. She watched as he spread on the disinfectant, then tore open a sterile gauze strip with his teeth. His face was hard, like granite, as he stared at his arm, intent on what he was doing.

They hadn't spoken about what had happened—or almost happened—on the beach, but she had set aside her longing, the day's sheer exhaustion dulling her emotions. So, he didn't want to go there. Fine with her. After the shock of the explosion, then almost drowning, she'd just wanted to feel a pair of strong arms around her. Even as she thought the words, she knew they weren't strictly true. She wanted to feel *his* arms around her.

She admitted her timing could have been better. Lying on a deserted beach in plain sight, with enemies on their tail, was hardly ideal for a tender moment, but his abruptness stung nonetheless. Still, she got the message. Loud and clear. Not interested.

Like she said, fine by her. She didn't need anyone compli-
cating her life, she'd had more than enough of that. Her bruised
heart couldn't stand to go another round, not to mention her
mental health. If she wanted to avoid danger, she was with the
wrong guy. Even though she knew he didn't bring this danger
to her. The reverse was true. This situation was all about her
and what she'd discovered. It had nothing to do with the
former Navy SEAL, who was only trying to keep her safe.

She watched as Phoenix struggled with the bandage,
dropping it twice.

Oh, for goodness' sake. "Let me."

His gaze shifted to her as she rose and circled the desk.
Leaning over, she gently wrapped the bandage around the
gash on his forearm, noting the flex of his muscles. He was,
in all honesty, perfectly sculpted.

In the flickering lantern light, he looked like some myth-
ical bronzed god, and her breath hitched. Being this close to
him, it was impossible not to feel a pull. Her hands trembled
as she secured the bandage. "There."

She made to step back, but he caught her hand. Her heart
went into overdrive, bouncing around her chest like a
jackhammer.

"Ellie—" His voice was a low growl, filled with pain.

She looked up into his tortured eyes, taken aback. "What's
wrong?"

He shook his head, his brow furrowed. "I can't… do this
to you."

"Do what? Hold me?" She searched his face, trying to
piece together the puzzle that was this man.

"I don't want to just hold you."

Then she understood. His need was as great as hers, but
he was afraid of where it might lead. She hadn't considered
the future. All she wanted was to feel his presence, to

confirm he was alive and with her. "It's okay," she murmured, facing him. "I'm scared, too."

He rose from the chair, towering over her. With a deep moan, he pulled her close, wrapping himself around her. She leaned into his chest, feeling his heart pound, his warmth driving away the fear, the anxiety, and the exhaustion.

In that moment, her world merged with his. As they clung to each other, she realized that while he exuded strength and confidence outwardly, he was terrified internally—not for himself, but for her. He didn't want to cause her pain.

"You deserve better," he murmured into her hair. "Better than me. I'm damaged, Ellie. You don't want this."

She looked up into his eyes. "You're exactly what I want. After the explosion, I thought I'd lost you. It terrified me. You're the only one looking out for me. Damaged or not, you saved my life. How can I ask for more than that?"

When their eyes met again, his were filled with a molten intensity, and she knew there would be no rebuke this time. She cared nothing for his past, only for what he was doing now. What he had done—for her.

He lowered his head, and his lips crashed against hers, consuming her. She felt an instant connection, a depth of feeling she'd never before experienced. Her body craved his touch, and he responded, intuitively knowing what she needed.

Her lips throbbed as he crushed against them, and as she opened to him, she felt like she was offering up so much more. She was exposing her most vulnerable side to him, her heart, but without fear. It could be in no safer hands. He was her protector—he'd said so himself.

Leaning into him, she sucked in a breath as his hard body moved against hers. His heat seared through her clothes, dirty and torn from the hike through the forest. His skin, scratched and torn, marred his perfection while making him seem more human. Human was what she wanted right now. She wanted to know the real him, not the protective outer covering he used to keep everyone out.

Her body ignited as he attacked her mouth with his tongue. Gasping, she held onto his broad shoulders, feeling the tendons moving under her fingertips as he grasped her and crushed her against him. He was devouring her, his tongue delving with deep strokes, showing her what it was like to really be kissed—no, to be *consumed*.

Fire burned in her belly and spread through her limbs, right to her core. All rational thought vanished as she gave herself up to the delicious sensations radiating through her. She arched into him, moaning against his mouth, growing wetter by the second.

A window creaked and he froze.

She held him, her heart still pounding. "What is it?"

"I heard something."

A tidal wave of fear washed over her. "Is it them?"

"I don't know. Keep down, I'll take a look."

He extinguished the lantern, and they were plunged into darkness. Ellie held her breath, listening for anything that might signal danger. Her body was hot, so tuned into him, to everything she was feeling, that she was on high alert. Her every sense aroused.

He slunk around the cabin, peering out of the windows. At last, his broad shoulders relaxed. "It's only a raccoon."

"Are you sure?"

"Yeah, I saw it run off. We're good."

"Thank God."

He came back over and sank down beside her, their backs against the wall. "You're trembling."

She bit her lip. "I thought it was them, that they'd found us."

"Too soon," he whispered. "They'd have to get back to the mothership and regroup. It would take time. I'd estimate they're at least a couple of hours behind us, more if you take into account the darkness, and the fact they won't know which part of the island we swam to, or if we even made it."

"Do you think they've found our inflatable?"

"Maybe. It could have washed up onto the beach. Either way, I'd say we've got some time." His slanted blue gaze bore down on her. "We should probably get some rest."

"I'm not tired," she murmured. She could still taste him on her lips. Salty, masculine, a sweet elixir that she longed to get more of. Her body was still tingling from his touch.

"Ellie…" It was a guttural whisper.

"Please, Phoenix. I need to feel you, to know you're there." Was that too much to ask? They might not even make it through the night. She didn't want to die without knowing what it felt like to be with him, to be consumed by him. She'd had a taste of it, and it was addictive. She wanted more. Much more.

"I've done things, Ellie," he rasped, his face twisting with pain. "Bad things."

"What things?"

He sighed and leaned his head against hers. She felt his pain, his angst, and she wanted to soothe him, to make it go away, but she had to know… "What have you done?"

He shook his head like it was too awful to talk about.

"Tell me," she whispered.

He took a shuddering breath. "It was last year, in Basra." His face filled with pain again. "God, Ellie. You don't need to know this."

She nodded encouragingly. "I want to know." She wanted to know all about him, about what had made him into the broken man he was today. Why he left the Navy SEALs, why he was on that rig in the middle of the ocean, tormented by demons he couldn't let go. It was part of who she was, her curiosity, her need to figure things out, to find a solution. Maybe there wasn't one here, but she still wanted to find out about the man she'd fallen for.

The thought made her inhale sharply. Yes, she'd fallen for Phoenix in a big way. She couldn't hide it anymore. She was head over heels for the guy.

He squeezed his eyes shut, as if digging deep within himself, then he opened them.

The anguish in them made her chest tighten.

"It was a messed-up situation. We'd gone in to rescue a bunch of women and children who'd been held hostage in an encampment. The terrorists were using them as pawns, to protect themselves."

As human shields. She fought back a shiver of familiarity.

"My team went in first. Butch and Slick were the first men in. They took out several hostiles, but then more came in from a back room. We didn't know they were there. Must have been in a bunker or something, out of range of our infrared scopes. The rest of us were shepherding the civilians out when we realized they had Butch and Slick at gunpoint. It was either them or the hostages."

She stared at him, horrified. The thought of violence and war were so far from her reality, it felt like he was describing a movie. She could only imagine the horror he must have felt.

"What did you do?"

"I knew they were dead, no matter what." His voice caught, and he swallowed. "Those bastards weren't going to let them go. So I made the decision to move the civilians out."

He paused, his face twisting in pain. When he spoke again, his voice was a whisper. "I abandoned them."

She grasped his hand. "It wasn't your fault. You saved the women and children."

"I left my men to die."

She held him then, cradling his head against her breast. He didn't cry, but she felt him shudder, and then his arms wound around her. There was desperation in his gaze as he looked up at her. He needed solace too, and she wanted to give it to him. She wanted to ease his pain.

"Ellie," he groaned.

"I'm here."

He snaked a hand around her neck and brought her head down to his. He kissed her, tenderly at first, then filled with need. Soon, she was gasping for breath.

They slunk down onto the hard cabin floor, but she hardly noticed the discomfort for he pulled her on top of him. Ellie wound herself around him, while he ravished her mouth again.

This time there was no stopping them. She could feel his need. Literally. His dick was thick and hard underneath her, pushing through his shorts and digging into her stomach.

Damn, she wanted him inside of her. It would be so easy to peel off her shorts, straddle him and—

She felt a surge of longing so deep it took her breath away, accompanied by a slick wetness between her legs. His hands gripped her butt, pressing her down, revealing every dip and bulge of his body, hard and solid under hers. God, she wanted him so bad.

Suddenly, his hands were under her shirt, sliding up her back, tugging the material gently over her head. Ellie lifted her arms and ducked, letting him pull it off. Panting, he fixed his hungry gaze on her, turning her stomach to mush. She felt desperate, like she was out of control—a sensation she usually hated.

Except this was different. This was exciting, exhilarating and terrifying all at the same time. It was insane how much she wanted him. Never before had she felt desire even remotely like this. Usually she was so clear-headed, so logical, so scientific. This was raw and spontaneous and totally out of character for her.

What could she say? Phoenix brought out her inner wild child.

He lifted his head and kissed her neck, his lips closing over her skin, hot and wet and unhurried, working a path along her collarbone and down to her breasts. She gasped as her bra popped loose, and she realized he'd unclipped it from the back. His gaze dropped to her breasts, now hanging free.

"Christ, Ellie. You're beautiful."

She didn't have time to reply, before he reached up and captured a hard bud in his mouth sucking it gently.

Holy hell.

She gasped, spiraling out of control. There was something so decadent, so erotic about his hot tongue on her nipple, that she nearly came right there and then. It was like he'd ignited a fuse that burned right to her core.

Moaning, she leaned forward, giving him more of her. His hands caressed her back, gentle yet insistent, tracing her curves with his fingers. She clawed the wooden floor on either side of his shoulders, moaning with ecstasy.

Beneath her, he grew bigger and harder, until she was straddling his cock, feeling it pulse between her legs. Any moment now and she was going to lose it entirely.

"Phoenix," she groaned, rubbing her groin against his. "Please… I need you."

He growled and tugged at her shorts. Lying on top of him, she undid the zipper, her hands trembling with anticipation. As soon as it was open, he shimmied them down, and she wriggled out of them. Her panties followed, already soaked with her desire. She reached for his waistband, and he reared up, nearly bucking her off. As soon as she had her balance, she stood, straddling him to tug off his shorts. When she got them over his knees, he managed to kick them off, then he pulled her on top of him.

There was nothing between them, but it still wasn't enough for her.

He lifted his head, his voice tense. "Ellie, I want you so bad, but are you sure?"

She'd never been so sure of anything in her entire life. "Yesss." It was a moan, a desperate hiss.

"Are you safe?"

She nodded. She'd been on the pill with Rafael and hadn't seen the need to go off it. "No problems there."

He grabbed her hips and positioned them over his cock. She was trembling so hard, he had to guide her down onto it. For a fleeting moment she wondered if it was going to fit. She hadn't been with many guys, and he was… huge.

She didn't have to wonder long.

Oh. My. God.

She'd never felt anything so incredible in her life. He filled her completely, thick and throbbing, and she closed her eyes, absorbing the entire length of him. She had to sit up, straddling him, to accept his full length, and for a moment, they both stared at each other, dazed at the overwhelming sensation.

Then he began to move.

CHAPTER 26

*H*oly shit, she felt good.

As her tight warmth enveloped him, all logical thought flew from his brain. Pure instinct took over.

She was so hot and slick and ready for him, his need catapulted out of control. He wanted this woman more than anybody he'd ever been with. Straddling him, her hair all wild like that, her glorious breasts catching the moonlight, Phoenix had never seen anything so beautiful.

Right now, in this moment, she was all his.

The possessive thought shot through his head, as he gripped her waist and began to move slowly beneath her. When she moaned, he knew she felt it too. Even if it only lasted one night, even if this was it, in this one moment, they belonged to each other. Solely and completely.

He slid in and out of her, slowly and smoothly, each time burying himself to the hilt. God, she felt incredible. He increased the pace, wanting more friction.

Ellie moved her hips in time with his, her mouth open in ecstasy, her breathing erratic, cheeks flushed.

He took a shuddering breath. He still couldn't believe she

wanted him, desired him, despite what he'd told her—and now here she was, giving herself to him in the most primitive way possible.

As their tempo increased, a tightness built inside of him, and all the tension, the hurt, the guilt began to recede, replaced by a molten heat in his balls so hot it was almost unbearable.

Fuck, he was flying, higher and higher, the ache growing stronger with each thrust. He fought back a sob as he gripped onto her hips, feeling her anchor him.

She ground against him, her movements becoming more frenzied.

She cried out, desperately. "Oh, God, Phoenix!"

He drove upwards, plunging into her, every thrust a balm on his shattered soul. The pressure grew until he couldn't stand it anymore. Everything he'd suppressed for so long mingled with his imminent release, and it was too much.

"Ellie—" He couldn't hold on much longer. Any moment she'd send him flying over the precipice, out of control.

Her body glistened with perspiration. She clutched at his chest, riding him like her life depended on it. He clung to her, making sure she felt every inch of his yearning.

"Oh. God. Phoenix. I'm gonna come!" A few more frantic thrusts and she screamed as her body convulsed around him. Her internal muscles clenched as her orgasm hit, and she gripped him like a velvet vice.

Any hope he had of holding on vanished, and he catapulted over the edge. A guttural cry escaped him as raw, hot lava exploded inside of her. Oh, sweet Jesus. He was drowning... floundering... emptying himself into her. He was vaguely aware of her bucking on top of him as wave after wave crashed down on him.

Holy shit.

She collapsed on top of him, panting hard, as the waves of

ecstasy turned into ripples, then finally, he stopped trembling.

He held her quietly, his breath mingling with hers, both of them spent. It didn't matter that they were both slick with sweat, that she was lying on top of him on the hard floor. He just didn't want to let go.

At that moment, he knew no matter what happened out here on the island, he had to keep this woman—his woman—safe. He had to make sure they survived, because he didn't want to let her go. Not now, not ever.

PHOENIX'S EYES SNAPPED OPEN, instantly alert. A foreign sound had jolted him from sleep—something out of place. Unnatural. The hairs on the back of his neck stood on end as he peered into the inky darkness. Disentangling himself from Ellie, he sat up, every sense straining.

There it was again.

The crack of a twig snapping under a boot—his early warning sign. The rustle of leaves displaced by stealthy movement. His hand crept to the shotgun.

They were here.

Despite the precaution of extinguishing the light and positioning themselves out of view, the shabby log cabin stuck out like a beacon for their pursuers.

Damn, he thought they'd have more time. He'd assumed the densely wooded terrain would delay an attack until daylight, but he'd underestimated their prowess, or was it their desperation? Either way, someone very clearly wanted them neutralized, and weren't prepared to wait.

"Ellie, wake up." He gave her an urgent nudge, then reached for his shoes. "Get up and get dressed—fast. They've found us."

"What?" she mumbled groggily, then gasped as the words sunk in. "They're here?"

He gave a terse nod.

Ellie yanked on her clothes and shoes, then huddled against the wall, out of sight. Her wide eyes tracked Phoenix as he risked a glance out the window. Two armed shadows glided across the clearing.

He waited but didn't see any more. Only two men to take out an ex-soldier and a scientist. Their mistake.

The ruthless game plan was obvious—perforate the cabin, then storm in guns blazing to eliminate any survivors. He knew, because that's what he'd do. It was fast, aggressive, and if done with an element of surprise, very effective.

Except he'd seen them and knew what they were up to.

"What do we do?" Ellie breathed, voice tight with fear.

"We need an exit route."

"You barricaded us in! There's no way out," she said, an edge of panic creeping in.

"The rug. Check under it." He gestured tensely. Ellie scrambled over and flipped back the worn rug, releasing a soft gasp.

"A trapdoor!"

"Yeah. That's how we'll get out."

She heaved at the wooden door. "It's stuck."

Phoenix lunged over and wrenched it open with a prolonged creak. He froze, listening hard for any reaction outside.

Poking his head down, he nodded. "It's all clear. You go first."

She shimmied through the rectangular hole and lowered herself onto the ground below. He followed, lowering the trap door behind him, just as a hail of gunfire erupted overhead, splintering the cabin walls.

"Make for the trees!" Phoenix whispered. "Don't look back!"

She wriggled out from under the cabin then sprinted for the tree line. Within seconds, she'd disappeared into the foliage.

Gritting his teeth, Phoenix veered in the opposite direction, blending into the undergrowth flanking the cabin. There was only one way to handle these guys, and that was to take them out.

He crept through the brush, ignoring the whip of the low-lying branches, until he was parallel to his target. The shotgun's blast would be too loud, and he didn't want to alert the other mercenary, so he drew his hunting knife instead.

Silently, he crept up behind the stocky shooter. The man had the build of a fighter, his military vest bristling with spare magazines. No doubt about it—these were hired killers.

The merc's rifle fire masked Phoenix's approach, but then, sensing rather than hearing Phoenix's presence, the shooter spun around.

Too late.

Phoenix's blade was quick and deadly. He clamped a hand over the man's mouth, muffling his scream as the knife severed his jugular. The rifle clattered away as the body slumped to the ground.

In the sudden silence, he knew it was only a matter of time before the guy's partner came to investigate. Phoenix grabbed the corpse by the ankles and dragged it into the dense underbrush, concealing it beneath a mound of leaves and branches. It wouldn't fool them for long. But every second counted.

Next, he retrieved the fallen merc's AK-47. Now armed with the rifle, shotgun and knife, the odds were tipping in his favor.

Phoenix turned his focus to the second mercenary. Ducking low, he moved silently through the trees and shrubs, circling to the other side of the clearing.

The second shooter had quit firing now. Phoenix studied him from behind the trees. He was taller than the other guy, with pale hair that gleamed in the moonlight. Not great for undercover work—too noticeable.

"Conrad?" the blond mercenary called. He had an accent that Phoenix couldn't place.

Hearing no answer, he advanced cautiously into the clearing, scanning for threats with obvious skill. This guy was no amateur.

The merc halted at the bullet-riddled cabin and peered through a shattered window. "Where are you?"

PHOENIX SIGHTED DOWN THE AK-47, finger poised on the trigger, waiting until the man stepped away from the cabin.

Two shots. A lethal double-tap.

The blond crumpled to the ground, dead before he hit the earth.

Although he was pretty sure these guys had come alone, just to be safe, Phoenix pulled the body into the jungle and hid it along with the other one. He scooped up the second rifle, checked the magazine, then slung it over his shoulder.

"Ellie!" He strode into the clearing. "You can come out."

Her ashen face emerged from the foliage, the lightening sky giving her an ethereal glow.

"It's okay," he told her. "We're safe now."

"Thank God!" She ran to him, only to skid to a halt, gaping at the bullet-ridden cabin. "Holy shit... they did do that?"

"Yeah."

She hugged herself to stop the tremors. "If we'd stayed in there—" She couldn't finish.

"Which is why we didn't." He moved toward her.

"Where... where are they?" She glanced around fearfully.

"Dealt with."

Ellie met his gaze, voice trembling. "They're dead, aren't they?"

At his nod, she swallowed hard, clearly struggling with the implications.

"I had no choice," Phoenix said, needing her to understand. He was no cold-blooded killer. "It was us or them."

"I know." She managed a weak smile. "I know you did what you had to. To protect us."

He exhaled and pulled her tight against his chest, savoring her warmth and softness. If only they could go back to how they were last night, entwined, basking in the afterglow of their lovemaking. The thought of danger far from their minds.

She clung to him, her heart hammering against his chest. The urge to protect her overrode his desire to hold her and comfort her any longer. They needed to move out.

"These guys must have a boat moored somewhere," he murmured. "I suggest we head down to the beach, locate the boat, and get the hell out of here."

When she looked up at him, her eyes were wet with tears. "That sounds like a great plan."

They salvaged what supplies they could from the ruined cabin—bottled water, some snacks, the first aid kit—then struck out downhill. This trail was wider and more worn than yesterday's, but he hoped it would lead them to the shore.

Ellie stuck close as they proceeded through the forest. It was hot and humid, and soon they were both perspiring.

After a grueling hour's hike, they emerged onto a sandy beach not unlike the one they'd first arrived on.

"There!" Phoenix pointed toward a rocky spit that curved out into the glittering turquoise water. At the end, a sleek speedboat bobbed against the rocks.

"Oh, thank God." Ellie grasped his hand. "Come on!"

"Easy," he warned, squeezing her hand, then releasing it. He needed both hands free in case he had to discharge his weapon. "Stay behind me and let me check it out first."

With a nod, she fell in behind him and they picked their way cautiously over the sand.

The boat looked nearly identical to the one that had fired on them yesterday after the oil rig explosion. It was obvious that whoever was behind this had serious resources. And more hired guns on tap, if those two thugs at the cabin were any indication.

"So far so good," he assured Ellie, as they clambered over the rocks toward the moored speedboat for a closer look. "I think we're in the clear—" The distant thwup-thwup of helicopter blades made the words to die in his throat. His head snapped up, eyes narrowing at the growing black speck in the sky.

"Is that the Coast Guard?" Ellie said, hopefully. "Billy must have informed them we're still missing."

Could be. They'd have worked out this was the nearest island and were doing a fly-by to check it out.

Then... the chopper banked hard and dropped altitude. Phoenix's gut clenched. Rescue pilots didn't maneuver like that.

"Ellie, get back!" he roared over the rotors' growing thunder. "Back to the trees, hurry!"

"What is it?" she cried, confused. "What's wro–?"

His desperate warning died as a man leaned from the

open helicopter door, assault rifle in hand, and let loose a hail of bullets.

CHAPTER 27

*E*llie charged after Phoenix along the rocky spit, stumbling over the stones, slipping and sliding in her haste to find cover.

What the hell was going on?

She screamed as a bullet pinged off a rock inches from her leg, spraying sharp granite shards.

The gunman in the chopper kept up a relentless barrage, stitching the speedboat with bullets until he found the fuel tank. The boat exploded in a massive fireball, lifted clear of the water by the force of the blast.

She stifled a sob. Now there was no way off the island.

"Don't stop, keep moving!" Phoenix barked, grabbing her hand. He pulled her toward the cover of the trees lining the beach in a desperate attempt to get away from the deadly rain of lead. By some miracle, they made it to the underbrush unscathed, the shooter forced to hold fire as the helicopter wheeled around for another pass.

"Are you hit? Let me see." Phoenix's eyes raked over her, checking for injuries.

"No, no. I'm okay." Her breathing was ragged, but she wasn't hurt.

He examined her like she was the most valuable thing on the planet. Even in this danger, she warmed at his concern.

"Thank God. We need to get deeper in, under heavier canopy." Together, they moved further into the forest. The dense foliage quickly closed in, bushes and trees weaving together until the sky had vanished completely.

"Now they'll be firing blind," Phoenix said, glancing up at the leafy roof.

Ellie stared into the damp tangle of vegetation, trying not to imagine what creepy-crawlies also sheltered there. Then she decided she didn't care. Whatever they were, the men with guns were infinitely more dangerous.

Phoenix zigzagged through the vegetation, changing direction every few yards. "It'll make it tougher for them to track us."

When he finally paused, Ellie sank gratefully to the leaf-littered ground, her muscles trembling with spent adrenaline.

The shooting had stopped. The chopper had gone ominously silent, too. But Ellie wasn't foolish enough to believe this was over. The killers had simply landed to continue the hunt on foot. They wouldn't quit until the job was done.

Until she was dead.

A sob caught in her throat. Phoenix immediately turned to her.

"Are you okay?"

"Are we going to die out here?" She hated the way her voice trembled with fear.

He dropped to his knees and engulfed her in a mammoth hug. "No, Ellie. We are not going to die here. I promise you that."

She sniffed. "You can't promise that. You're just one guy. They've got a helicopter full of mercenaries. Oh, God."

Don't panic. Breathe.

Panicking would only slow them down. She had to hold it together.

Phoenix was silent. That worried her even more than his optimistic promises.

"Have some water." He shrugged off his pack and passed her a water bottle. She gulped gratefully, using it as a way to catch her breath.

"How much time do we have?" Her question quavered only slightly.

"Not much."

"I should never have taken this job," she said bitterly. "I was an easy mark, simple to manipulate and dispose of. Stupid, naïve—" She pressed shaking hands over her face.

Phoenix squeezed her shoulder. "Shh. I think they're close."

Ellie swallowed her words.

Sure enough, the faint rustle of disturbed vegetation drifted to her ears, punctuated by the heavier crunch of combat boots.

"Stay down and don't move, no matter what. I'll come back for you." Phoenix guided her under the sheltering fronds of a massive fern.

"Don't go!" Her fingers locked around his wrist. She was suddenly terrified to be left alone. Please..."

"I have to. But I will come back, I promise." He covered her hand with his. "Ellie, look at me. You need to trust me now, okay?"

She did. God help her, she did. Throat tight, she managed a nod.

"That's my girl." His lips brushed hers in a fleeting kiss.

Then he was gone, melting into the shadows without a sound, leaving her huddled and hardly daring to breathe.

* * *

PHOENIX DISAPPEARED INTO THE JUNGLE, checking his weapon as he went. He had about twenty rounds in the rifle and another fully loaded magazine in his pocket, courtesy of the second merc at the cabin.

Should be enough to do what needed to be done.

Grimly, he set the AK-47 to semi-automatic mode. He wanted to conserve ammo and not expend the magazine unnecessarily.

He gave their pursuers a wide berth, circling around them out of sight. He wanted to see what he was up against before making any moves. He kept low and crept stealthily through the bush like he'd been trained, his movements absorbed by the spongy undergrowth of the jungle floor—unlike his attackers, who were making more noise than a troop of monkeys. They obviously figured with more boots on the ground and superior firepower, they had the upper hand. Well, Phoenix didn't know how many times he'd disproved that theory over the course of his career.

Gotcha.

He crouched low, invisible amongst the darkly leaved bushes, and watched. Three men, all dressed in jungle fatigues and armed with bullet-proof vests stuffed with ammo. They'd come prepared. There'd be a fourth man, the chopper pilot, who'd be waiting on the beach, ready for the exfil.

The man in front—tall, rugged, and graying at the temples—looked to be in charge. He issued a sharp command, then the three men split up.

Phoenix exhaled under his breath. Perfect. They'd be

much easier to neutralize one by one if they weren't hunting as a pack.

He stalked the third man as he walked through the overgrown jungle, his bald head moving from left to right like a radar, listening for any sign of movement. He was about to make a move, when he felt a hand on his arm.

Shit.

He swung around, ready to strike, but found himself looking into Boomer's grazed face.

"Holy shit," he cursed, under his breath. "I nearly took you out."

Boomer gave a soft snort. "You didn't even hear me coming."

It was true. He hadn't. He'd been so intent on his target, he'd neglected to cover his six. He squeezed Boomer's arm, silently acknowledging how goddamned happy he was that his friend was still alive. "Great to see you, buddy. I could use some backup." There was a large scab on the left side of his face, and several deep cuts on the right, but he was alive. That's all that mattered. Explanations as to how the hell he'd survived the bomb blast could wait. Right now, they had a mission to complete.

Phoenix signaled the direction of the remaining hostiles. Boomer nodded, slinking away into the shadows.

Time to focus on the hostile up ahead. The mercenary was built like a bull terrier, short and stocky with a barrel chest, but Phoenix had the height advantage.

With a burst of speed, he closed the distance, utilizing his height advantage to grab the merc from behind. In a fluid motion, he pulled the man's head back and sliced his throat. The merc gurgled, clutching at his neck before collapsing.

He never even saw his attacker.

Phoenix removed the man's blood-soaked Kevlar vest and slipped it on. It was filled with extra ammo, including a hand-held grenade that might be useful later. Then he turned and went to find Boomer.

It didn't take long.

He found his buddy standing over the body of another mercenary. Like the bald guy, this one also had his throat cut and was bleeding out on the forest floor.

"Good hit," Phoenix commended. "Two down, one to—" A scream turned his blood cold. "Ellie!"

They charged back to her position, diving for cover as bullets tore through the foliage. Each thud of a bullet against the trees felt like a hammer on Phoenix's chest.

"Hold fire!" Phoenix shouted, raising his rifle. His voice was steady, but he couldn't still the frantic beating of his heart. "I'm coming out."

Boomer melted into the underbrush like a shadow, while Phoenix slowly stood, gut wrenching at the sight of Ellie kneeling before the gray-haired merc, a pistol to her head. Her eyes were wide with terror, tears streaming down her cheeks.

"Lose the weapon."

Phoenix complied, tossing his rifle aside, feeling a pang of helplessness as it clattered to the ground. Even though Ellie was whimpering, he kept his eyes glued to the merc's. One sign that he was going to pull the trigger, and he'd attack—to hell with the consequences.

"Let her go," he rasped, his voice barely concealing the fury bubbling beneath the surface.

"Sorry, can't do that." Phoenix knew that already, but it had been worth a shot.

"Who hired you? Was it Xonex?"

He sneered, "What do you care? You'll be dead in a minute."

"Then why not tell me? Satisfy my curiosity."

A snort. "A group called Gilded Futures. I don't know who they are, only that they pay well."

Gilded Futures, he'd never heard of it, but Ellie obviously had. She gasped, her hand flying to her mouth, her eyes wide with shock and recognition.

"I see you know them, sweetheart." The merc traced Ellie's face with his gun. She flinched, squeezing her eyes shut, but somehow managed to keep it together.

Two shots shattered the tension. The merc crumpled forward, his grip on the pistol slackening. Ellie scrambled away, her breath coming in ragged gasps.

Phoenix surged toward her, gathering her into his arms. "I've got you. It's over." She clung to him, her body trembling with great sobs. She'd been through so much. He held her tightly, feeling the warmth of her tears soaking through his shirt, as Boomer emerged from the shadows, his face a mask of grim determination.

"Thank you." Phoenix's gaze locked on Boomer's. He'd saved Ellie's life, and probably his too.

His friend nodded. "You'd do the same for me."

He would have. That much was true.

Ellie gasped and spun around. "Boomer! You're alive. Oh, my God. You're really alive?"

He chuckled, the sound almost foreign in the tension. "Yeah, although at one point I didn't think I was going to make it."

"How did you?" Phoenix asked. "I saw that bomb go off. I thought it was game over."

"It was a directional charge, rigged to blast upwards to target the structure. That's how I managed to escape the worst of it," he said. "Not to get too technical, but when the charge blew, I threw myself behind a bulkhead. The force was massive—enough to knock me out cold, but the bulkhead shielded me from shrapnel and the worst of the shockwave."

"You're lucky you didn't drown," Ellie breathed, her voice a mix of awe and concern.

"The cold water hit me like a wall, jerking me back to consciousness. I floated, disoriented, until I grabbed onto some debris."

"How the hell did you get here?" Phoenix asked, still holding Ellie close as if she might disappear if he let go.

"The other lifeboat was still intact," he said. "Or mostly intact. I plugged a few holes and rowed here. I knew the island was only a couple of miles out, I'd seen it from the chopper on the flight over."

"Amazing," Ellie breathed. It was good to see her smiling again, even if it was small and fleeting.

Phoenix squeezed her hand. "What do you say we get the hell off this island?"

"There's a fourth merc on the beach," Boomer warned. "Guarding the chopper."

Ellie's face fell, the brief glimmer of hope fading.

"Don't worry," Phoenix told her, lifting her chin so she met his eyes. "We've got this." He and Boomer exchanged a look, a plan already forming between them. The resolve in their eyes said it all: they were getting off this island, no matter what.

Phoenix held Ellie's hand as they crept through the dense jungle behind Boomer, his senses on high alert. Peering through the final line of trees, he spotted the helicopter on the beach under the watchful eye of the last mercenary.

"We need to neutralize him quickly and quietly," Phoenix whispered. "I don't want to risk him alerting anyone else."

Boomer nodded, his jaw set in grim determination. "I'll circle around and approach from the left. You take the right. We'll catch him in a pincer move."

Phoenix turned to Ellie. "Wait here. I'll be back to get you, I promise."

She squeezed his hand, then released him with a whisper. "Be careful."

With a silent nod, the two ex-SEALs split up, melting into the shadows of the jungle. Phoenix moved like a ghost, his footsteps making no sound on the soft earth. As he approached the edge of the tree line, he slowed, scanning the beach through the foliage.

There.

The mercenary stood beside the helicopter, his rifle held loosely across his chest. He looked bored, unaware of the danger closing in on him from two sides.

Phoenix waited, his muscles coiled and ready. Down the beach, he knew Boomer was doing the same.

A bird call pierced the air—Boomer's signal. Phoenix burst from the trees, sprinting low and fast across the sand. The mercenary spun, trying to bring his rifle to bear, but Boomer was already on him, a silent shadow attacking from behind.

The mercenary crumpled under Boomer's chokehold, his rifle falling uselessly to the sand. Phoenix kicked it away, then helped Boomer lower the unconscious man to the ground.

Boomer checked the mercenary's pulse. "He's out cold, but he'll live."

Phoenix allowed himself a grim smile. "Let's tie him up and get out of here before he comes to."

Together, they bound the mercenary's hands and feet with zip ties from his own vest, then gagged him for good measure. Phoenix did a quick sweep of the helicopter, ensuring there were no tracking devices or booby traps.

"All clear," he reported. "I'll fetch Ellie and we can get the hell off this island."

Boomer grinned. "Roger that."

CHAPTER 28

*S*he buckled up as the chopper took off, with Phoenix at the helm and Boomer beside him, leaving the unknown barrier island behind. The remaining bad guy was trussed up next to her, still out cold. Served him right for trying to kill them.

The helicopter ride reminded her of the first time she'd flown out to the Explorer—filled with excitement, hopes, and dreams. Ellie scoffed. What a fool she'd been. If only she'd known then that they'd hired her only to take advantage of her... and to easily dispose of her should the need arise.

Thank God for Phoenix. He'd saved her life—in more ways than one.

She admired the back of his neck as he flew the chopper, operating the throttles and equipment like he'd been doing it all his life. How could he be so calm? Only moments ago, he'd admitted he'd only flown a couple of times before.

Somehow, he always managed to make her feel safe.

She marveled at how different he was to Rafael. Rafe had only shown her a toxic form of love, laced with uncertainty and fear. Thanks to him, she'd hidden herself away in Scotland, preferring the sanctuary of an isolated oil platform rather than real life. This job had been the same, until she'd met Phoenix.

It was insane how much had happened. In the last two weeks, she'd been almost swept off a rig, blown up, drowned, attacked by a shark, and stranded on a deserted island. Not to forget the team of mercenaries hired to kill her.

And somewhere amidst all that, she'd fallen in love with an ex-Navy SEAL. A man who'd repeatedly put his life on the line to save hers. A man who would die to protect her.

Her eyes stung with tears, not of sadness, but of hope, gratitude, and love, but she blinked them away before anyone noticed.

They banked, and she turned to look out of the window at the azure blue ocean far, far below. There was still the matter of who was trying to kill her and why. But she wanted to enjoy this moment, this slice of freedom for a little longer, before they had to think about what to do next.

WHEN THEY LANDED in Corpus Christi, Texas, they were met by two more men just like Phoenix and Boomer. They were both tall, broad shouldered, and drop-dead gorgeous. Honestly, where did they find these guys?

Ellie could tell straight away they were both ex-military. Something about the way they held themselves, that quiet confidence that Phoenix had in spades, and the reserved smiles that held so many dark secrets.

After the backslapping and hand shaking, Phoenix introduced them as Pat and Blade.

Pat's eyes crinkled as he grinned at her. "Good to meet you, Ellie. We heard you guys might need some backup." She guessed he was in his early forties with salt and pepper hair and a handsome, rugged, face. As Ellie gazed into his steely-gray eyes, she found herself warming to him. He exuded strength and competence.

"I think we're going to," Ellie replied, trying not to show how relieved she was to see them. They needed all the help they could get to take down the organization behind this.

"When we heard about the explosion, we jumped on a plane as fast as we could," said Blade, who could have been made of granite, he was so chiseled.

"Appreciate it." Phoenix thumped him on the shoulder.

"Who's that?" Blade pointed to the semi-conscious mercenary in the chopper.

"One of the guys who tried to kill us," Phoenix said. "We're going to turn him over to the authorities."

They called the Coast Guard, who were involved with the oil rig's clear-up operation, and explained what had happened. They, in turn, called the police. As expected, there was a ton of red tape to get through, but after she'd given her statement, Ellie let Pat and Blade take her back to their hotel.

Phoenix and Boomer, it seemed, still had a lot of explaining to do since they'd left three dead mercenaries on the barrier island and had a fourth, semi-conscious one in tow.

"They'll be okay," Pat told her, clocking her worried frown in the rearview mirror. "After what's happened, they're going to have to give statements about the IED they found on the rig as well as what happened on the island."

She nodded, unsure what to make of these two hulking men who Phoenix had entrusted her to. She hadn't missed the curious glances they'd been giving her since she'd landed in the chopper.

"How'd you meet Phoenix?" Blade asked conversationally, as they drove toward the hotel.

"On the Explorer," she said, figuring it was too long a

story to start at the beginning. "After the bomb went off, I pulled him out of the water. He was concussed and bleeding, but we managed to get to the island where we found shelter and medical supplies."

"Lucky for you," Pat said.

"Is that when the hit squad found you?" Blade asked.

She cringed at the term, and saw Pat elbow him in the ribs. "There were two of them. They'd followed us to the island, I'm not sure how. Phoenix… dealt with them, and we escaped to the beach to see if they had a boat waiting, but that's when the others arrived in the helicopter." She took a shuddering breath. Four men, including the pilot. Phoenix said they were mercenaries hired by the organization responsible for all this."

"Does this organization have a name," Pat asked.

"Gilded Futures LLC. That's who hired the hit squad, as you put it. We don't know who they are or what they do, but we think my boss, the man who hired me, is part of it."

"What makes you think that?" Pat glanced at her in the mirror.

She took a shaky breath. "I think he hired me on purpose, hoping I'd be too inexperienced or intimidated to question the anomalies in the test samples. That way, nobody would have found out about the falsified survey reports until much later."

"Huh?" Blade spun around, his brow raised.

"Oh, sorry. I forgot you don't know what I'm talking about."

She filled them in, starting with the fake geographical data and ending with the IED. She even told them about the attempt on her life during the storm, when Billy had been knocked overboard.

"They're trying to cover their tracks," Pat said, and she could see his forehead was deeply furrowed.

"Most of my evidence was lost in the explosion," Ellie told them. "I don't have anything that can prove the reports were faked, or that my samples were useless."

Saying it out loud made her heart sink. If they couldn't prove any of it, how were they ever going to catch these guys?

"Well, the Coast Guard and relevant authorities have launched a full-scale investigation into the oil rig explosion," Blade told her. "Maybe they'll find something."

"I hope so," she murmured, feeling the tension of the last few hours weigh down on her.

They pulled into the hotel parking lot. Ellie stared up at the gleaming high-rise and then at her filthy attire and cringed. "I can't go in there looking like this."

"I've got a clean shirt if you want to wear that," Blade offered.

"Okay, thanks." It was something, at least.

Ellie changed into it in the car—it was like a dress, reaching her all the way to her knees. Coming up with a plan, she asked Blade if she could use his belt, and buckled it around her waist.

There, that wasn't so bad.

Hopefully nobody would notice her filthy tennis shoes.

"Are you okay to share a room with Phoenix?" Pat asked, casting a sideways glance at her.

She flushed, but nodded, her heart doing a funny little flip at the thought of sharing a luxurious hotel room with Phoenix.

"It's probably best you don't check in under your real name, just in case they've got people out looking for you."

That was a sobering thought. He must have sensed her trepidation, because he put a hand on her arm. "Don't worry, we're right next door if you need us."

"Thanks, Pat." He was a sweet guy, for a former SEAL Commander.

"And tonight," Blade added, sticking his hands in his pockets. "We'll figure out how we're going to deal with these guys once and for all."

"You really think that's possible?" She didn't miss the look that passed between him and Pat.

"Oh, you can count on it."

CHAPTER 29

*H*oly hell.

The first thing Phoenix saw when he let himself into the hotel room was a sleeping Ellie, dressed in nothing but a man's white shirt, her legs bare. She lay on top of the massive bed, her freshly washed, still damp hair spread out over the pillow. She looked like an angel.

A fucking sexy angel.

If he wasn't so exhausted, he'd have taken her into his arms right there and then and removed that shirt, especially as he was pretty sure it was exactly like the one Blade had been wearing earlier.

On top of the exhaustion, he was filthy and probably didn't smell too good after two days in the jungle. Peeling off his soiled clothing, he tossed it into the corner of the room then stalked, naked, into the bathroom. Seconds later, he was luxuriating in the best shower he had ever experienced—or at least it felt that way.

The police questioning had been intense, and they'd kept him and Boomer there for nearly four hours, verifying every last detail of their statements. Finally, they'd been allowed to leave but were told not to go far.

One thing he had managed to discover was that they were still going through everything found at the wrecked rig site. So far, forensics hadn't managed to figure out what had caused the blast—or who. But with Boomer's accurate description of the IED and Phoenix backing him up, they would be able to refocus their search in the right place.

As for the lab equipment, electrical devices, and reports, it didn't look like anything had survived, and anything they retrieved from the water would be damaged by now.

After emerging from the shower, he dried himself off then lay down next to Ellie on the bed. It was big enough that they didn't touch. Phoenix pulled a sheet over himself, seeing as he was naked, but the thought of putting on his dirty clothes was not appealing. The hotel room was nice and cool, the blinds drawn. Ellie's breathing beside him soothed his galloping mind, and soon he was dozing off.

PHOENIX DIDN'T KNOW how long he'd been sleeping when he felt Ellie stir. He was about to drop off again, when he felt her roll over and snuggle up beside him. A slender arm draped over his waist, and he felt soft breasts under the shirt press against his side.

Oh, boy.

Any notion he had of going back to sleep evaporated as his body sprang to life. He couldn't help it. She was so beautiful, so angelic with her wild hair, and her shirt riding up to expose her long, pale thigh and a hint of perfect butt.

He ran a hand down her arm, making her shiver. Then her eyes fluttered open and her delighted gasp made his dick turn to granite.

"Phoenix, you're back."

Was he ever?

Ellie draped a leg over his, and even though he was under the sheet, he felt her heat burning right through him. Turning onto his side, he wrapped an arm around her slender frame and kissed—hard.

A gasp caught in her throat, then she leaned into him, her breasts crushing against his chest, her leg intertwining with his, pulling the sheet with it. Soon, they were a tangled mess of limbs and arms and desire.

When they broke for breath, he kicked off the sheet then rolled on top of her, pinning her beneath him. She felt much smaller than he remembered, probably because in the cabin on the island, she'd been straddling him. Suddenly he was aware of his weight. "I'm not too heavy, am I?"

She shook her head, her eyes dancing. "I like it."

Goddamn, she was sexy. Flushed cheeks, lips swollen from kissing, breath coming in excited little gasps. His dick jerked in agreement. It was all he could do not to ravish her right then and there.

One thing he'd realized at the police station was Eleanor Rider, chemical engineer, could never be his. Not really. The best he could hope for were moments like these. The questions they'd asked had been an eye-opener.

"How do you know Miss Rider?"

"Did you know she was a chemical engineer?"

"Did she discuss her work on the Explorer with you?"

"Where was she during the explosion?"

At first they'd suspected Ellie was involved, but he'd told them about her discovery, about how she'd questioned the validity of the reports, and how she herself had been targeted on the Explorer, narrowly escaping with her life. That, along with her trip to the Discoverer to double-check the geographical survey maps seemed to satisfy them. While they'd have more questions, she was off the suspect list.

It made him realize how different they were. She was smart, ambitious, a scientist. He was a blunt instrument, the only thing he knew how to do well was kill people.

She was integrity and intelligence.

He was lethal.

Like oil and water, they'd never mix. Once this was over, he'd go back to work for Pat and the team at Blackthorn Security, while she'd go on to her next job on some other oil field somewhere in the world, far away from him.

It was probably for the best, even though thinking about it had made him feel physically ill. Still, if that was their future, right now he was going to make damn sure she never forgot him.

Slowly, he unbuttoned her shirt. Those big, cat-eyes fixed on his face, brimming with anticipation. "I'm going to show you what it's like to be loved," he murmured, bending his head and sucking one of her nipples into his mouth.

She gasped, and thrust upwards, arching her back.

He gripped her under her ribs and worked his tongue and teeth until her nipple formed a hard, granite nub, then he moved to the other one.

"Oh, God." She squirmed beneath him. "That feels so good."

He was just getting started.

Kissing his way down, he inserted his fingers under the edges of her panties, feeling her twitch beneath him, before he peeled them off. She was soaking wet, which made his cock throb with longing.

In the cabin, it had been rushed, frenetic, their desire taking over, their coupling tinged with danger and an urgency he knew came from a first time together. Now, he wanted to linger, to draw out every second. To make her scream his name as she came so many times she'd think she'd died and gone to heaven.

She rose off the bed, pushing her groin against his hand. Gently, he rubbed his fingers against her wetness, hearing her sigh at the touch, then moan as he delved deeper, his finger finding its mark. At the same time, he kissed the gentle curve of her stomach, her hip bone, and the soft hair around his finger.

"Please…" It was a throaty whisper as she thrust up and down against his finger. Next thing, it was inside her, sliding in and out, stroking her until she cried out with pent-up desire. He moved faster, rubbing his thumb against her enlarged bud, little circles that had her crying out his name.

"Phoenix… Oh, God. Oh!"

He replaced his thumb with his tongue and licked and sucked until she came, shattering beneath him with a strangled cry. He held her steady as she arched her back off the bed, unwilling to release her until every last ecstatic wave had rolled through her.

CHAPTER 30

*S*he was flying… falling… dying.
Finished.

Breathing hard, she stared at Phoenix in awe. What the hell had just happened? Her entire body was trembling, and yet she still wanted more. How could that be?

He'd literally just shattered her, and now he was kissing his way back up.

Wrapping her arms around his neck, she drew him close, her whole body pulsing with aftershocks. He held her, murmuring in her ear, nibbling her neck, and then claiming her lips once again.

This time, he possessed her mouth with his tongue, thrusting, sucking, showing her just how much he wanted her. There was no mistaking his desire, as his enormous erection pushed into her thigh.

God, she was so ready for him!

He'd made her so wet, she was practically dripping—not something that had ever happened to her before. Somehow, her body just responded to this man, melting under his touch.

Wrapping her legs around him, she whispered, "Take me. Take all of me."

His midnight-blue eyes scorched into hers, as he positioned himself on top of her. Bending his head, his tongue delved into her mouth as he rolled his hips forward then thrust into her in one swift stroke.

She cried out against his mouth, but he sucked the sound out of her, burying himself so deep that she could feel him touching her cervix. It was almost enough to send her over the edge again.

He exhaled in a hiss as he withdrew, before sliding in again, filling her so completely that she convulsed around him. How was it even possible that she was coming again so soon? One more thrust and she was gone.

His balls against her skin, her body absorbed every inch of him. She cried out as he took her over the edge, then he held her, staying deep within her as she shuddered beneath him. Her insides pulsed with a release deeper and more satisfying than she'd ever experienced before.

Sweet Lord.

Overcome, she felt hot tears slide down her face, but he kissed them away. When she'd stopped coming, he pulled back, then thrust again, his own desire taking over. Gripping onto his shoulders, she felt him increase his pace until she was once again rocking beneath him.

Oh, shit.

She was going to come. Again!

Matching his increasingly violent thrusts, she felt herself riding a wave that got bigger and bigger the harder he drove into her. She was rising off the bed, the headboard slamming against the wall, masking the sound of their skin slapping together.

Part of her thought he was going to split her apart, but the other part cried out, "Yes, harder. Oh, God. I'm coming!"

She heard him give a low yell as he slammed into her, flooding her with his scorching seed, possessing *all* of her—over and over again.

It was too much.

Ellie screamed as her orgasm hit. Her insides clenched around his swollen cock, feeling him pulse into her, throwing her off the cliff and into the abyss. She came hard, unable to help it. Hands clutching at his shoulders, hips raised off the bed, legs holding him in a vice-like grip, she broke into a thousand shards of glass, totally shattering beneath him.

ELLIE WALKED into the bar convinced the other men would know what they'd been up to. She was pretty sure she was still glowing. How could she not after *that*?

Phoenix.

Oh, God. She felt her pussy twitch just thinking about him. He'd made her come multiple times until she was a shaking, whimpering mess and he was spent, panting beside her.

Before they'd come downstairs, they'd gotten Blade to get them a change of clothes from the hotel clothing store. Consequently, Phoenix was wearing blue jeans and a T-shirt with a bull's head on it and Texas scrawled in a vintage font across the top. It wasn't his usual style, but she thought it kind of suited him, particularly the way his rock-hard thighs filled out the denim.

"What do you call that?" he'd glared at Blade, as he'd handed Ellie a thin, silver slip dress, silk pantyhose and heels to match.

"You said to get her something nice." He shot Phoenix a wicked grin.

"It's fine," Ellie giggled, taking it from him. The only

problem was she'd put it on, just to have Phoenix peel it off again, which was why they were late.

"'Bout time," growled Pat, gesturing for them to sit down.

"You look very nice, Ellie," Boomer said, winking at her.

"Thank you, Boomer." She smiled back and sat next to him. With a sour look, Phoenix took the remaining chair.

Pat, Blade, and Boomer were drinking beers, so they ordered two more from a passing waiter then got down to business.

"We did some digging into Gilded Futures," Pat began. "They're an investment firm specializing in commodities and futures markets. On the surface, they look legit."

"Except we know they're not," Ellie cut in. "They hired those thugs to kill us."

"If they're behind this, they bribed a survey company to falsify records in order to convince Xonex, a private energy company, to acquire expensive drilling licenses and start exploratory drilling in a location that held no oil reserves."

"Do you know why?" Blade asked.

Phoenix shook his head. "Could be any number of reasons."

"Who did you say was involved?" Pat asked Ellie.

"My boss, a man called Henderson. He works for Xonex."

"Okay, we'll get our people to look into him." Pat took out his phone and fired off a text message.

It was nearly eight o'clock, and he still had people working for him? Ellie was impressed.

"How are we going to catch them?" she asked. "Phoenix and I are the only loose ends, and they don't know where we are."

"Not yet," Blade said, the corners of his mouth turning up.

Phoenix scowled. "I don't want Ellie involved in this. She's been through enough."

"Okay," Pat said slowly, "But we're going to have to make them think she is, else they won't come."

"Come?" Ellie looked between Pat and Phoenix, confused.

"We're going to set up a sting operation," Blade explained for her benefit. Somehow, the other men already knew what they were going to do. "We need to draw them out."

"Which means we have to make them think you've got evidence that can get them arrested," Boomer finished.

"Like what?" Ellie said. "I lost everything in the explosion."

"But they don't know that," Phoenix told her. "You were out on the inflatable when the rig went up. Henderson saw you return, that's how they knew to come after us."

"So?"

"He doesn't know you didn't have your laptop with you, or some other incriminating evidence."

Ellie nodded slowly. "How are we going to convince them that's true?"

"Do you know anyone at Xonex you can call?" Pat asked. "A friend, maybe."

"There's Suzi." She glanced at Boomer and then Phoenix. "She left to visit her father the morning of the blast. I could call her and tell her I managed to get away with my laptop with everything on it and need to convince the authorities of the fraud."

Boomer frowned. "You think they'll be tracking Suzi's phone?"

"Maybe," Phoenix said, thoughtfully. "Ellie could tell Suzi she wants to get a message to Henderson, as she's worried about her job and wants to know what she should do with the information."

Boomer tensed his jaw. "You're going to use Suzi to contact Henderson?"

"He's her boss too," Phoenix said, reasonably.

"I'll just act like the clueless bimbo they always wanted me to be." Ellie gave a determined nod. "After all, that's why they hired me. Shouldn't be too hard to convince him I'm lost and don't know what to do with my reports, which belong to the company, anyway."

Pat grinned. "Sounds like a plan to me."

Phoenix inhaled, his giant chest rising. "Where's she going to say she's staying? Not here."

"Another suite," Pat said. "They have some chalets out by the golf course. She can say she's in one of those. They're relatively isolated, easy to get to unnoticed. Fewer security cameras."

Phoenix was nodding.

"I'll ask for one right now," Ellie said, standing up. "Then I'll make the call."

The sooner this was over, the better.

"Brave girl," she heard Pat say, as she walked away. Phoenix's reply was lost in the general chatter of the bar.

He wouldn't have said that if he'd seen her two weeks ago. She'd been a simpering wreck, too scared of her own shadow to do anything even remotely risky. Then Phoenix had dive-tackled his way into her life, and all that had changed. Now she felt empowered, like she was doing something proactive.

Hell, she was still terrified—that hadn't changed—but at least she was dealing with the fear now, not quaking in her boots, unable to breathe.

Ellie booked the chalet by the golf course then returned to the men. They were bent over the table, talking in low voices, their massive shoulders all huddled together. It was quite a sight.

"Ready?" Pat asked, looking up.

She nodded. "Ready."

"Okay, make the call."

Boomer handed her Suzi's number, and she used Pat's phone to call it.

Suzi answered almost immediately.

"Suzi, it's me, Ellie."

She listened while her friend screamed into the phone. "I thought you were dead. I've been trying to call you. Oh, my God, Ellie. What the hell happened?"

"I lost my phone," she began honestly. It had been left on the inflatable when it had sunk. "But I've been meaning to call to let you know I'm okay."

"Where have you been?"

"I managed to make it to a nearby island, and I was rescued from there this morning. I'm in a hotel in Corpus Christi now."

"Which one? I'll come and see you. Are you all right?"

"Yes, I'm fine. Honestly, there's no need to come. I'm actually calling to ask you a favor."

"Oh?"

"I need to get hold of Henderson."

A pause came before Suzi spoke. "Henderson? Why would you want to get hold of him?"

"Well, he's still my boss," she said, as if that was obvious. "And I've got my reports and laptop with me with all my findings on them. They're Xonex's property. Now that the rig is… well, destroyed, I don't know what to do with them. I'm guessing we no longer have jobs."

Suzi let out a little sigh. "I can try and call him for you, but I don't know if he'll pick up. The company is getting a lot of heat right now."

"I understand." She glanced at Phoenix. "Well, if you could try him once more, I'd appreciate it. He can call me here at the hotel."

"Where are you staying?"

"At the Palmetto Sunset Hotel on the waterfront. I have a chalet by the golf course. I'll be here for a couple of days before I decide what to do."

"Okay, stay put, and I'll be in touch."

They said goodbye, and Ellie hung up.

"How's that?" She glanced at Phoenix, whose eyes were shining.

"You did great."

"Brilliant," agreed Pat. "Now let's hope she gets in touch with your crooked boss."

"I feel bad using her." Ellie bit her lip.

Boomer nodded. "Me too."

"It's the only way." Phoenix reached for his beer. "At least now we've planted the seed. We'll hide in Ellie's chalet and wait for them to arrive. When they do, we'll catch them red-handed."

"What about me?" Ellie asked.

"You'll be in our room, out of harm's way," Phoenix said, decisively. Ellie knew there was no point in arguing with him. She'd done her part, now it was over to them. There was nobody more capable than these four men. If they couldn't take down the next hit squad Gilded Futures sent after her, then nobody could.

CHAPTER 31

*I*t was a warm, quiet night. Phoenix couldn't even hear a rustle from the trees on the golf course surrounding the cabin. It would make it easier to hear them coming.

They'd used a simple trick, scattered Rice Krispies around the perimeter so they'd hear when the bad guys approached. Phoenix was inside the cabin, while Pat and Blade flanked it, and Boomer was hidden out of sight further down the road to provide early warning if anyone approached.

Now it was just a waiting game.

Time stretched endlessly, but on ops like this, it always did. He remembered once waiting nearly forty-eight hours for a high-value target to show at a remote compound in the arid outskirts of Kandahar. The target was a terrorist known for orchestrating devastating attacks across the region.

Phoenix recalled how—as the hours ticked by—the landscape had transformed with the setting sun, casting long shadows over the dry and dusty Afghan terrain. It was during those twilight hours the target had finally appeared— and they'd taken him out.

The hardest part was staying focused for all that time, keeping your breathing steady despite the adrenaline pumping through your veins. It was like that now. Hunkered down behind the door, out of sight of the windows, not moving a muscle.

When the hostiles finally entered the cabin, he'd spring into action, backed up by Pat and Blade, with Boomer cutting off their escape route.

They'd asked the hotel for a manilla folder, which they'd filled with blank printer paper and placed on the coffee table in the center of the room. It was pretty obvious, but these guys would be expecting to find something, so they had to dangle the bait.

It would also draw their attention, meaning they'd be distracted, making it easier to subdue them.

"Don't take them out unless there's a clear and present danger," had been Pat's orders. They didn't engage in unnecessary use of force, no matter how tempting it might be. Phoenix gritted his teeth and thought back to how that one merc had held a gun to Ellie's head. He could still see the terror in her eyes, the tears running down her pale face.

A surge of something intensely protective gripped him, making him tense. He never wanted her to experience such fear again. Nobody should have to go through that, let alone after the trauma she'd suffered in her past.

Which was why they could never be together. Despite what had happened—was happening—between them, Phoenix knew it could only ever be temporary.

This was his life.

Hiding in shadows, taking out targets.

With him, she would always be afraid. If not for herself, then for him. Wondering if he was going to come home safely to her.

He couldn't do that to her.

Phoenix pushed the depressing thought to the back of his mind. There were things to do first before he had to cross that bridge. A hit squad to neutralize, and a corrupt organization to take down.

Then he heard it. The faint snap, crackle, and pop of the Rice Krispies. Simple, yet effective.

"Contact," he murmured into his comms. Pat had equipped them all with state-of-the-art earpieces for secure communication.

"Roger that," whispered Blade.

"Negative contact on my side," whispered Boomer, which meant the hostiles must have approached across the golf course. Right now, he knew Boomer would be moving to cut off their escape route, while Pat and Blade would be closing in from the flanks.

Then everything happened at once.

The door flew inwards, breached with a portable battering ram. These guys were professionals. Two masked men entered in a tactical stack, weapons at the ready. They scanned the room, one gestured to the other, then they moved deeper into the house.

"Freeze," whispered Phoenix, pressing the muzzle of his suppressed Glock against the back of one of the intruders' heads.

The man froze, his arms going up.

"Don't move a muscle, or it'll be the last thing you do."

The man complied.

Silent as a wild cat, Blade slunk up behind the other intruder. There was a brief scuffle, then a thud.

Two down.

Outside, they heard a muffled pop and exchanged glances. That was a suppressed gunshot, which none of them had fired.

"I'll check it out," Blade darted back outside, leaving his suspect zip-tied on the floor in the main bedroom.

Phoenix cuffed his suspect, then secured him to a chair before going to restrain the one Blade had knocked out.

More shots rang out, and Boomer dashed in, clutching his shoulder. "Goddamn it. Henderson shot me."

"What? Henderson's here? Are you okay?"

"Yeah, it's just a through-and-through. Pat's in pursuit. He's going to need backup."

Knowing he was no good as a shooter with his injury, Boomer stayed to guard the suspects while Phoenix took off after Pat. Blade was nowhere to be seen.

"Blade, come in?" Phoenix called over the comms. He only got static in response. He tried again, then Blade's voice came through, garbled and broken. "Suspect is heading toward the ninth fairway... I'm cutting him off at the dogleg... Need backup... Over."

Shit.

Phoenix had gotten the gist of the fragmented message and made his way around the putting green, keeping to the tree line until he reached the ninth fairway. There, he saw Pat chasing Henderson, who zigzagged across the fairway like a pro soccer player. The oil boss was fit.

No way he was getting away. Phoenix charged out from behind the trees. He tackled Henderson on the fringe, sending him flying then lunged after him. The two men grappled on the ground.

Phoenix wrenched the gun out of Henderson's hand and tossed it into a nearby bunker, out of reach.

"You bastard," Henderson muttered. "I knew this was a sting."

"Surprised you showed up then," Phoenix growled, pinning him down on the rough. The man was crushed under his weight, but Phoenix didn't ease up. In fact, he might have been intentionally making the murderous scumbag even more uncomfortable.

"I came to see what trap you'd laid for my men."

"Your men? I see. Now I know who's calling the shots."

A snort.

Pat came running up the fairway. "Bastard gave me the slip." His gray eyes were almost luminous in the dark. Pat didn't take kindly to being outmaneuvered. None of them did.

"It was easy. I knew you'd go for my guys, which is why I sent someone up to the hotel to look for your little girlfriend." Henderson snarled at Phoenix.

His blood ran cold.

"What?"

"You don't think I figured she'd be here, did you?" A sneer crossed his face.

Phoenix gripped him by the collar, pressing him into the rough. "What have you done to Ellie?"

"What do you think? She knows too much, which means your little girlfriend is going to have to die."

Was he bluffing? Phoenix didn't know whether to believe him or not.

"Go," Pat said, taking custody of Henderson on the edge of the fairway. "Go to her."

"You're too late," Henderson smirked, his chuckle following Phoenix as he sprinted across the course, making a beeline for the hotel.

CHAPTER 32

*E*llie was just getting into bed when there was a knock on the hotel room door. "Who is it?" she called. It couldn't be any of the men. They'd only just left.

A familiar voice said, "Ellie? Can I come in?"

Suzi!

Ellie sprang out of bed and opened the door. "Oh, my God. Suzi, what are you doing here?"

Her former colleague gave her a hug, then walked into the hotel room, closing the door behind her. She looked different. On the rig, she'd worn cute little dresses, but now she was wearing distressed denim jeans with holes in the knees, a Metallica T-shirt, and big, clunky boots. Her eyes were rimmed with black eyeliner, and the stud in her nose was now a small hoop.

"I had to come and see you," she said. "I had to make sure you were okay."

Ellie was touched. "Thank you, but you really didn't need to come all the way to see me. A phone call would have been fine."

"So, what happened?" Suzi asked, perching on the edge of the bed. "Tell me everything."

Where to start?

"It was awful." Ellie told her about the explosion. "I was coming back from the Discoverer when the oil rig blew up. It was like this massive fireball in the sky. I couldn't believe what I was seeing."

"Terrible," murmured Suzi.

"Thank God Billy managed to get the remaining staff members into the second inflatable. Otherwise, there would have been multiple fatalities. As it was, we nearly lost Boomer and Phoenix." She shook her head, her eyes filling with tears at the memory. She didn't think she'd ever get over that.

"They're okay?" Suzi asked.

"They are now, but it was touch and go for a while there. Phoenix had a concussion and scrapes and bruises, but Boomer nearly got blown up. He was unconscious for a while, and his face got all messed up."

"Poor guy," Suzi said. "Serves him right for meddling like that."

"What?" Ellie stared at her, confused by the reaction.

Suzi released her hand. "I really like you, Ellie, but you know what your problem is? You ask too damn many questions."

Ellie stared at her for a long moment. Slowly, the pieces fell into place. "No," she finally whispered. "Not you too."

Suzi rolled her eyes. "Well, of course me, stupid. How else were we going to position the rig at those coordinates? Any geologist worth a dime would have recognized the difference in morphology if they'd looked at a chart of the seafloor. I'm not that dumb."

Holy shit.

Suzi.

As the horrifying truth sank in, several anomalies began to make sense. Like why Suzi had left the morning of the blast. "Your father didn't have a bad fall, did he?" she asked.

"Of course not. My parents are long dead. It's just me and Jasper."

"Jasper?"

"My son. He's ten."

"I didn't know—"

"How could you?"

Ellie gawked at her, still unable to believe her roommate, a woman she thought was a friend, was capable of this. "How could you risk all those lives?"

"I tried to get everyone off," Suzi said. "I told Henderson to order two helicopters that morning instead of the usual one. It could have been much worse."

Ellie didn't know what to say.

"Plus, I got you off, didn't I?" Suzi added. "You were supposed to get rescued and go home. Instead, you stayed around to speak to the authorities."

"They came after me," Ellie hissed, finding her voice. "Whoever blew up the rig sent a team of mercenaries after me to finish the job."

Suzi sighed. "I know, and I'm sorry about that. It's not the way I wanted it to be, but I'm afraid I didn't have any say in the matter. You knew too much, so you had to be silenced."

"Who got to you?" Ellie asked after a beat. "Who made you do this?"

Suzi stood up, her hands trembling. "You don't know what it's like, Ellie. My son, he's sick. He needs constant medical care, and the bills just keep piling up. I've taken out loans, maxed out my credit cards, but it's never enough."

Ellie's heart sank. "Why didn't you say anything? I could have tried to help you."

Suzi gave a snort. "What could you have done? You

weren't in any better situation than me. We both got the job because we were young and inexperienced. I could be manipulated into using forged survey reports, and you should have just done what you were supposed to and kept the operation going."

"Why?" Ellie asked again. "Why did they want to keep it going when there was no oil?"

"You're so naive. Henderson and his organization were making a killing on the markets. News of a potentially lucrative discovery in the eastern Gulf. Investors were falling over themselves to get a piece of that pie."

"They were going to sell before Xonex pulled the plug on the drilling operation?"

"Six months, and Xonex would announce there were no reserves. Mass panic. The share price would fall, but they'd be out by then."

"It's appalling," Ellie whispered.

"It's a game," Suzi said. "You wouldn't have been affected anyway. Not much. You'd get another job somewhere else. This would just be a blip on your resume. You don't have to worry about choosing between paying for your child's medication or keeping a roof over your head."

"They offered to help with the medical bills?" Ellie said, edging closer to the door. If she could just get past Suzi and make a run for it, she'd have a chance at calling for help.

Suzi couldn't prevent her eyes from welling up. "They said they'd take care of everything. All my debts, the medical bills, even set up a trust fund for my son's future care. All I had to do was help them with this one thing."

Ellie shook her head in disbelief. "But at what cost, Suzi? You've destroyed so many people's lives, their careers."

"I had no choice," she snapped. "It was either that or watch my son suffer. What would you have done, Ellie? If it was your child?"

Ellie fell silent, her mind reeling. She couldn't even begin to imagine the desperation Suzi must have felt. "I don't know," she whispered. "But there had to be another way."

Suzi laughed bitterly. "Easy for you to say. You've never been in my shoes. Never had to make the choices I've had to make." She reached into her handbag, her eyes hardening. "But none of that matters now. What's done is done."

Ellie's eyes widened as Suzi pulled out the syringe. "Suzi, what are you doing?"

"I have to finish what I started."

Panic surged through her veins, and Ellie felt herself go numb. Not again. Please, not again. "You don't have to do this."

"I'm sorry, Ellie," Suzi's voice was ice. "But I do. They'll take everything from me if I don't. My son... I can't let that happen. I won't."

Ellie stared at the syringe in Suzi's hand. It was half-full of a clear liquid. "You're going to inject me?"

"I'm finishing the job," Suzi said. "You're the last loose end. You and that good-looking boyfriend of yours. But don't worry, Henderson's taking care of him."

"It was Henderson who set the bomb, wasn't it? It was him I saw speeding away that day when I was returning from the Discoverer."

"Well deduced, my friend." Suzi took the cap off the syringe.

"Help!" Ellie shouted, scrambling for the door. "Somebody help me."

Suzi pushed her onto the floor. For a small woman, she was remarkably strong.

"Shut up," she spat. "No one's coming. Your soldier body-guard is on the other side of the complex."

Ellie gripped her wrist to prevent her from injecting her

with whatever was in that syringe, but Suzi was too strong. The needle came closer. "Suzi, stop. This is madness."

"You shouldn't have asked for those satellite images," Suzi snarled. "You could have just done your stupid job, and none of this would have happened. But you had to poke your nose in, didn't you? You had to find out the truth, and now look where it's got you?"

With a final heave, Suzi jammed the needle into her arm.

Ellie screamed and tried to fight Suzi off, but it was no use. Suzi had pushed down on the syringe, and Ellie felt the needle pierce her skin.

Suddenly, the hotel room door burst open, and Phoenix charged in, his eyes blazing with a fury Ellie had never seen before. His face was contorted with rage, a vein pulsing in his temple as he took in the scene before him. "Get away from her!" he roared, his voice raw with emotion as he lunged at Suzi.

Suzi jumped back, startled by the sudden intrusion, and as she did so, Ellie managed to whip out the syringe—but it was too late. Some of the liquid had already entered her bloodstream, and she could feel it beginning to take effect.

Phoenix grabbed Suzi by the arms, his grip so tight it was sure to leave bruises. He slammed her against the wall with such force that the pictures hung nearby rattled on their hooks. "What did you do to her?" he demanded, his voice a low, menacing growl. Ellie had never seen him like this before, his usual calm demeanor completely shattered by the sight of her in danger. His eyes were wild, almost feral, as he glared at Suzi with a look that could only be described as murderous.

Suzi struggled against his grip, but Phoenix held her fast.

"Phoenix…" she murmured as her vision began to blur, and she felt her limbs growing heavy. She tried to finish her sentence, but her tongue wouldn't cooperate.

Phoenix threw Suzi against the wall so hard she crumpled into a heap on the floor. Then he rushed over to help her. "Ellie? Ellie, stay with me!"

But she couldn't. Her eyes were closing.

"What was in that syringe?" Phoenix demanded, turning back to the dazed Suzi. "What was it?"

His voice was so loud, echoing in Ellie's head.

"You're going to tell me exactly what it was," Phoenix snarled, as Ellie fought the darkness creeping in from the edges of her vision. She could hear his voice, but it sounded distant, as if he were calling to her from underwater. She tried to fight the heaviness pulling her under, but it was too strong.

Just as she was about to slip away, she felt Phoenix's arms around her, lifting her from the bed. "Stay with me, Ellie," he pleaded, his voice breaking. "I can't lose you. Not now. Not like this."

He held her close as he carried her out of the room, shouting for someone to call an ambulance. Ellie forced her eyes open, struggling to focus on his face.

"Phoenix," she whispered.

"I'm here, Ellie. I'm not going anywhere. Just hold on, okay? Help is coming."

Ellie tried to nod, but it was too much effort. She just had to close her eyes, to sleep for a while. She was so tired.

"Ellie, stay with me," she heard Phoenix say, but she couldn't.

Not anymore.

With a sigh, she gave in to the darkness.

CHAPTER 33

*P*hoenix found himself praying as he gripped Ellie's hand and felt her pulse flutter weakly beneath his fingers.

Please don't let her die.

I promise I'll be the kind of man she deserves.

I'll protect her.

I'll make her happy.

His bargaining continued as the ambulance cut through the night, its sirens crying through the otherwise quiet streets. Ellie lay on the gurney, her face ashen, the steady drip of an IV the only barrier between her and death.

Phoenix watched the paramedics work calmly and quickly to stabilize her, administering oxygen and monitoring her vitals, keeping up a steady stream of medical jargon that he could barely follow.

His own heart pounded in his ears as the memory of finding Ellie convulsing from the poison played on a loop in his mind. He should never have left her alone, never underestimated Henderson. Now, all he could do was hold her hand and hope it wasn't too late.

As the ambulance thundered toward the hospital, he leaned close, murmuring into her ear. "Stay with me, Ellie. Fight this. You've got to fight."

Outside, the city passed in a blur, the bright flares of streetlamps streaking by like falling stars. The ambulance maneuvered through the traffic with urgent haste, every turn and stop jarring them, but Phoenix's gaze remained fixed on Ellie, his grip on her hand unyielding.

He couldn't lose her too. Not after all they'd been through together. He'd known from the first moment he'd tackled her on the helipad in her yoga outfit that she was someone special. At first, he'd thought she was too good for him, but she'd convinced him that he was wrong.

He recalled the way she looked at him with awe, like he was some sort of hero because he'd been trained to save lives and to keep going no matter the odds. He couldn't believe he'd inspired her to be stronger, braver. To get over her panic attacks.

Truth be told, she made him feel like the man he used to be—and wanted to be again.

She made him feel like he was worthy of her love.

In the sterile, blinding brightness of the ambulance, with the sharp smell of antiseptic in the air and the cold touch of metal all around, his world narrowed to the sound of Ellie's strained breathing and the paramedics' steady efforts to save her.

His training had prepared him for many things, but not how to deal with the crippling helplessness of watching Ellie fight for her life.

PHOENIX PACED UP and down the corridor, the harsh fluorescent lights hammering his senses.

"Hey, buddy, we heard what happened," Boomer said,

running up to him. Phoenix gave him a brief hug, then turned to Pat and Blade, who'd come in after him.

"Thanks for coming."

Boomer's shoulder was taped up. "I'm here to see the doc," he said with a wry grin. "How's Ellie?"

"I don't know." It was fucking killing him. The medics had converged as soon as they'd entered, wheeling her off to God knows where to pump her full of antidotes. He only hoped it wasn't too late.

Thank God that bitch hadn't depressed the syringe more than a few millimeters, or else Ellie would be history. His stomach clenched. He couldn't even go there. Even now, he felt like a bystander in his own nightmare, powerless as they fought to undo the damage.

"What happened?" Pat asked.

"Suzi got to her. She was in on it the whole time."

Boomer balked at him. "Suzi? You're shitting me."

"No, man. I heard her say something about a sick kid before I blasted in there. She took a bribe to pay for his treatment or something."

Boomer shook his head. "Now that I think about it, it makes sense."

"How so?" Phoenix asked.

"She never said anything about a sick child, but she kept phoning home. Then there was the way she just up and left, taking the chopper back the morning of the explosion. I always thought that was lucky."

"Yeah, and she was the one who suggested to Ellie they go up on deck during the storm. That's when Ellie would have been swept overboard if Billy hadn't stepped in."

"Fucking hell," Boomer growled. "Why does it always happen to me?"

"You certainly know how to pick 'em," Blade remarked dryly.

"What happened with Henderson?" Phoenix focused on anything that would prevent him from freaking out with worry.

"He's in police custody," Pat said tersely. "Bastard's trying to cut a deal by giving up the other members of the organization."

"Typical," Phoenix grunted. "He deserves to rot in hell for what he's done."

"A representative from Xonex has arrived," Pat continued. "They're going to sue the survey company as well as Gilded Futures over the fake reports and corporate espionage. The damages could run into millions."

"Glad to hear it," Phoenix said, raking a hand through his hair. Shit, he really needed to know how she was doing. Had they gotten to her in time?

Was the antidote working?

He spun around as the doctor, a competent-looking woman in a white surgical coat, emerged. "How is she, doc?"

"We've successfully administered the antidote. Ellie is expected to make a full recovery," she declared.

Relief crashed into him, and he put one hand out against the wall. "Thank God."

Boomer thumped him on the back. "That's great news!"

Pat and Blade were both grinning from ear to ear.

"You can see her now if you'd like," the doctor offered, her hand warm on his shoulder.

He jumped up and followed her to Ellie's room. The heart monitor beeped a steady rhythm, a sound that was suddenly the most precious in the world.

Her eyes fluttered open as he entered.

"Hey." He took her hand. "You gave me quite a scare."

"Tell me about it."

He grinned. "How are you feeling?"

"I'm okay. The doc says I'm going to be just fine."

"That's so great, Ellie. I was so worried…" He broke off, emotion overwhelming him.

"I know. Thanks for bursting in when you did. How did you know?"

"Henderson," he explained. "Pat and the others caught him by the golf cabin."

"Thank goodness you came in when you did."

He choked out an apology. "Ellie, I'm so sorry I left you there alone. I should have been there to protect you."

"You can't be with me constantly," she admonished gently. "Besides, you didn't know she was involved. Nobody did. She fooled us all."

"I should have worked it out."

"Hush," she said, her voice stronger now. "You saved me, that's all that counts."

There she was, gazing up at him like he was a rock star. His heart surged, and he gripped her hand tighter.

"I couldn't stand the thought of losing you," he began, his words stilted. "Ellie, it made me realize… I love you. I don't know when it happened, but sometime over the last few weeks, I fell in love with you. I know you deserve better than me, but I just wanted you to know that."

She stared at him, a soft smile playing on her lips.

"You're my hero, Phoenix. You know that, right?"

He looked away. "But I can't make you happy. I'm a soldier. It's the only thing I know how to do. You hate danger."

"But I love you."

His head shot up to look at her. "You do?"

"Of course I do. You've made me realize I don't have to be afraid anymore. You've taught me that there are men out there who won't hurt you, who will protect you no matter what. That means more to me than any occupation you might have."

"So you're willing to look past it and… and be with me?"

She gave a soft laugh. "I'm very much looking forward to getting out of here so I can show you just how willing I am."

Phoenix leaned in and kissed Ellie. Once he started, he found he didn't want to stop.

"Excuse me, sir. You can't do that in here," a nurse interrupted.

Only then did he release her, stepping back as Ellie burst out laughing.

The nurse, trying not to smile, added, "I'm glad you're feeling better. You'll be discharged later today. Just need a few more hours to make sure everything's okay with your vitals and there's no nasty side effects from the poison."

"Thank you," Ellie said, a blush creeping up her cheeks.

Phoenix pulled a chair close, still holding her hand. The hospital room, with all its beeps and that clean, sharp smell, suddenly didn't seem so cold. He felt lighter, like he could finally breathe after being underwater for too long. For the first time since that mess in Basra, he wasn't looking over his shoulder. He was looking forward. Ellie had done that for him.

She was more than just the woman he loved. She was his salvation. Ellie had shown him he was worthy of happiness and could be the man he'd always aspired to be. With her, he felt like he could take on the world, like the past was just that —the past. The old ghosts would always be there, but they didn't define him anymore.

Leaning close again, this time mindful of the nurse still in the room, he whispered, "I love you. And I promise, I'm always going to be here for you."

Ellie's smile was all the reply he needed, her eyes lit up just for him. "I know," she whispered back. "Because that's who you are, Phoenix. My hero, my love, my everything."

* * *

WHAT'S NEXT?

Want more Blackthorn Security? Take a look at the next book in the addictive romantic suspense series.

SILK SHADOW

GEMMA FORD

SILK SHADOW

BLACKTHORN SECURITY - BOOK 3

A detached special forces operative with everything to lose. A feisty influencer used to getting her way.

When social media influencer and entrepreneur, Izzy, starts getting death threats, she turns to her mother's old friend, a military veteran who runs a private security company to help her. He assigns Viper, a new recruit, to be her personal protection officer. With abs harder than barnacles and eyes the color of the ocean, Izzy can't deny her attraction to the strong, silent bodyguard—but despite her best attempts to seduce him, he remains aloof.

Viper needs this job. He went off the rails after leaving the Navy SEALs and this is his one chance to forge a career for himself in the private security industry. Izzy wasn't quite the assignment he was expecting, but when she gets kidnapped during a fashion shoot, things suddenly get serious. Viper has to get her back if he's going to save her life—and his career.

This is a sizzling, edge-of-your-seat, bodyguard romance by Amazon bestselling author, Gemma Ford, with some steamy scenes. Available on Amazon and Kindle Unlimited.

CHAPTER 1

*V*iper arrived at Blackthorn Security headquarters in Washington D.C. at precisely 0900 hours. His shirt was crisp and immaculate, his suit, while not from Madison Avenue, was the finest he could afford. His shoes gleamed so brightly that he could see his reflection in them. He wanted to look the part. This was the most important meeting of his career, and he couldn't afford to screw it up.

"Don't worry, Pat's a good guy," Blade had told him during his surprise visit last week. "I served with his son over in Afghanistan."

Viper wasn't so sure. He'd heard that Pat was a hard man to get to know. Stubborn and unflinching when it came to picking and choosing their operations, absolutely incorruptible, and a force to be reckoned with. Rumor had it that he even made the smooth-talking politicians on Capitol Hill quake in their boots. A man to be admired, but it did make him rather formidable. But then, he'd expect nothing less from a former SEAL Commander.

Pat's reputation preceded him. He'd built Blackthorn Security into an organization steeped in secrecy and rumor.

His operatives were all ex-military, mostly spec ops, and they got the job done. Their success rate was through the roof, which was a lot more than could be said for most private security companies.

Viper had researched them thoroughly after Blade's visit.

Blade Wilson.

Now there was a blast from the past. He'd never thought he'd see that mountain of a man again, not since the SEAL's last op in Afghanistan where his entire team bar one had been taken out. After that, Blade had bailed on the military—medical discharge—and the last Viper had heard, he'd gone missing—presumed dead—in the Middle East during an off-the-books assignment.

"I thought you were dead," he'd told him through a God-almighty hangover, when his old acquaintance had appeared at his door a couple of days ago.

Blade had snorted. "Takes more than a few angry Taliban soldiers to put me down. I heard you were out and thought I'd pop over for a cup of joe. You going to invite me in?"

Viper didn't have much choice. Blade was blocking his doorway and didn't look like he was going to move any time soon.

"Sure, why not? I could use one myself."

"Rough night?"

Viper ran a hand through his disheveled hair and winced at the tender spot on the side of his head. He'd literally peeled himself off the couch five minutes ago.

"Nasty graze you got there. How'd it happen?"

"I think someone hit me over the head with a bottle," he complained, feeling it with his finger. "But it's a bit hazy."

Blade studied him. "Bar fight?"

A shrug. "Something like that."

They walked into the kitchen where Viper poured two

cups of coffee from a freshly made pot. He didn't even ask if he wanted cream, just handed it to him black.

No cream in the Middle East. They'd all gotten used to drinking it black.

Viper turned to face his buddy, still confused as to why he was here. "So, you were just passing through the neighborhood and thought you'd look me up?"

"Yeah, and I've got a proposition for you."

Viper sat down a little unsteadily. His head was pounding, but he couldn't decide if it was because of his hangover or the dent in his hairline. "A proposition? What kind of proposition?"

Blade sat opposite him at the kitchen table. "I heard you'd been making a bit of a nuisance of yourself." He'd always been very direct. Not one to beat around the bush.

"Who told you that? I was helping a damsel in distress. Some guy was laying into her. I just shoved him off." And got a bottle in the head as a screw you.

Blade glanced at the wound that Viper hadn't even bothered to clean up yet. It was still seeping, despite the scab beginning to form. "Something tells me he didn't appreciate it."

Viper winced. "You could say that. The cops didn't appreciate my good will either. Spent half the night in lockup."

Blade sipped his coffee contemplatively.

"What's going on, Viper?" he asked after a pause. "This isn't like you. You're a SEAL sniper for God's sake, you take out the enemy from a distance. You don't go around looking for bar fights."

"I told you, I was helping—"

"Yeah, I know what you said. It's just unlike you, that's all. Are you bored or something?"

Viper stared into his coffee, still gently swirling from where he'd stirred it. A long moment passed where he said nothing at all. When he finally spoke, his voice was a hoarse whisper. "I'm so freakin' bored, I'm thinking about putting a bullet through my head."

"Jesus, man. Why don't you get help?"

"Hey, don't panic. I'm not suicidal, not really. I just don't know what to do with myself. I thought about getting a job, but I'm not qualified for anything, except maybe working on the oil rigs up in Alaska. I don't want to be a fucking security guard at a shopping mall. This not knowing what to do is killing me." He ground his jaw and clutched his mug so hard he thought it might break.

"That's why I'm here," Blade said.

Viper glanced up.

"I've got a job for you."

He frowned. "Where?"

"Where I work, at Blackthorn Security."

"You work for *them*?" Everyone on the private security circuit knew about Blackthorn Security. Ex-Special Ops guys on off-the-book assignments for the U.S. government, as well as some private clients. Most of the time, they were talked about in hushed tones with a degree of reverence usually reserved for legends in the field.

"Yeah, I'm the Ops Manager. I started the company with Pat Burke after I got back from Afghanistan. I was in a dark place, and he came to me with his idea, and we took it from there."

Viper stared at him. "I had no friggin' idea, man."

"Not many people do."

"So, what does the esteemed Blackthorn Security want with me?"

"We have a job that requires your particular skill set, and we're pretty swamped at the moment. Business is booming and we're still recruiting operatives. There's a lot of bad crap going down in the world."

Viper scoffed. Blade didn't have to tell him that. He'd been involved in more than his fair share of it over the last decade.

"You've done personal protection work before, haven't you? I seem to remember you guarding those oil engineers out in Iraq a couple of years back."

"Yeah, although that was a sideline. A special favor for the Navy." He shrugged. "You know my skillset is somewhat different."

"I know." Blade gave a slow grin. "That's what makes you perfect for this job. We've got a client who needs close protection around the clock. She's a very important client, a personal friend of Pat's, and she's been getting death threats."

"Who is it?"

"Doesn't matter. It's a job. We could really use your help on this one, man. If all goes well, we'll sign you on full-time. Pension plan, dental, the works. We have ops all over the world. It's a great opportunity."

Viper hadn't had to think about it for long.

After Blade had left, he'd showered, gone to the nearest walk-in clinic and got three stitches in his head, then called Blade back and accepted.

ENJOYED THE EXTRACT? *Silk Shadow* is now available from Amazon and Kindle Unlimited here: www.amazon.-com/dp/B0D743CJ5F.

ABOUT THE AUTHOR

Gemma Ford is a romantic suspense novelist who enjoys writing about feisty, independent women and their brave, warm-hearted men. *Honor Code* is the second book in Gemma's Blackthorn Security romantic suspense series.

You can browse the rest of the series or sign up to Gemma's mailing list for discounts, promos and the occasional freebie at her website: www.authorgemmaford.com.